THE INNERVATIONS

A JOURNEY THROUGH THE PROBABILITIES

SUMEET S. NAVALKAR

ISBN 979-888591773-5

Contents

Prologue

This image and the coloured variant on the back cover are an approximate diagrammatic representation of the entire story.

CHAPTER I

Anekand had started his experiments quite early. He was only 31 when he had first managed to make the leap. The experience had been traumatic but he had felt jubilant once it was over. Traumatic because it was the first of its kind for Anekand, perhaps it was even the first for anyone. He was anxious that he would be lost in the infinite possibilities, but once he was back, his joy had been unmatched. Even though he had been successful, he was not sure he would pull such a stunt again without failure. But then once again, he had gathered all his courage and had done it. This time too he was successful. Then again and then again. With every success, his confidence had built up. After a few such successes, his anxiety decreased, and he considered himself proficient enough to make the leaps. This was not overconfidence though. He knew he didn't understand everything and perhaps he never would, but he was the only one with this kind of knowledge as far as he knew and so logically, because of no competition or comparison, he was by default- proficient. An year earlier, his sister had died. It was a murder. Anekand was so depressed that he didn't practise meditation for almost a year. It was almost unbelievable because people in depression usually started meditation, and he had quit doing that. He kept himself busy in the routine and mundane things of life. But a year later, he realised he couldn't live his life the way he was living it. And then he got back to his normal self- this time with more vigour. He wanted to understand it all and experiment with all the facets of meditation. He knew it was the only thing that would bring him out of his depression. And that's when those leaps started for him.

• • •

Murder:

That day, Anekand was going to return home early. His sister was already home from their office. Both worked in the same office, and that was because they owned it- family business. He was on a call when his sister left. Ten minutes later, he left too. Though they worked at the same office and went home to the same apartment, they drove their own separate cars. This was a mutual decision so that one would not have to wait for the other.

Anekand left the office as soon as his call was over. He was driving home. Somewhere on the way near a flyover, he noticed a brick lying somewhere on the road below. This road too reached his home, but he always took the flyover to avoid the signals. But today he had seen a brick on that road. Fearing that this brick if missed being seen by a motorcyclist would prove fatal to him, Anekand swerved his car away from the flyover onto the road below. He slowed down, stopped to a side and came out of his car. He walked up to the brick and kicked it away from the middle of the road towards its side. When he got back inside his car, his eyes fell on an envelope. He was going to drop that off into a post box. But now he had missed taking the flyover. The person he was going to send the letter to was a client and his office was on the way. So Anekand decided to drop off the letter personally.

Once at the client's office, the client called Anekand for the meeting there and then. In the end, when he left the client's office, he was already two and a half hours late than he would have been if he had taken the flyover. He took half an hour more to reach home through the evening traffic.

When he opened the door to the house, Anekand met with a gruesome sight. His sister was lying on the floor in a pool of blood. She was dead.

The police suspected Anekand for the murder because he seemed to have motive. He and his sister were the only heirs to the family business and with his sister gone; he would inherit the entire family fortune. But he had a strong alibi. He was with a client when his sister had been murdered. From the autopsy reports, Anekand knew that his sister had been murdered when he was still in his client's office. The problem, however, was that there was no other DNA found at the site of murder. There was also no evidence that could prove a forced entry into the house; there also wasn't any sign of struggle. All this evidence or lack of it pointed towards Anekand, but since he could not be at two places at the same time, he was acquitted.

To lose his sister was a shock to Anekand. Moreover, it wasn't a natural death- it was a murder. And as if it were not enough, Anekand was suspected of the crime. He loved his sister dearly and his sister loved him too, but emotions and feelings are locked in the mind and were invisible to those who wanted him for murder. It was an irony that to prove a false suspicion of love for money wrong, he could not use the fact that he loved his sister. Though he was acquitted, the experience had left scars. A year would pass by before Anekand would be Anekand again. For now, he was just routine (work-eat-sleep) trapped in a loop.

• • •

The Beginning:
Anekand had started yoga or meditation since he was 12. As he practised it, he started understanding how to transform his brainwaves and achieve states of mind that

were beyond most people. As he experienced these states, he started using meditation not only with the intention of controlling his mind and achieving inner peace, but for recreational purposes. It was similar to a person using drugs or chemicals for recreational purposes, but without the possibility of getting addicted to an external substance and abusing it in an unhealthy way. After around sixteen years of experimenting with and experiencing different states of mind, one day at the age of 28, Anekand had an even odder experience.

"Can you hear me?" said a voice as Anekand was deep in his yogic or meditative state.

He knew the voice he had heard wasn't through his ears. It had directly accessed his brain. Was he hallucinating? But Anekand didn't wake up from his trance-like state. He continued.

"Can you hear me?" the voice said again.

"Yes," replied Anekand telepathically.

"Great. That means I can communicate with you."

"And I with you," said Anekand. "But who are you?"

"I am consciousness."

"Whose consciousness?"

"That's a complicated question to answer."

"Complicated meaning I won't understand or you don't know?"

"Complicated meaning difficult to put in words."

"But if you are consciousness, then you don't need words," said Anekand.

"I suppose you are right. But I am new to this."

"You are new to this and yet you could communicate with me. I have around sixteen years of experience and yet I have never thought of it or done it. How many years of experience so you have?" asked Anekand.

"This is my first ever communication."

"OK. But for how many years have you been practising meditation?"

"Years? I don't know. I cannot measure time though I understand chronology. It may be a moment old or perhaps eons have passed. I don't have a sense of time myself. Time has its meaning to me only through you. So I don't know what you expect when you ask me my experience in years. But I can judge time through you, and so it must be billions of years. Yes, that seems to be the correct answer. It's more than ten billion years in the time you understand."

"What do you mean?" Anekand asked still in his meditative state.

"I may be eternal and infinite and though I don't understand time on my own, time cannot exist without me. I am time, I am you, I am everything."

At this point, Anekand snapped out of his meditative state. He could take it no longer. He opened eyes and blinked. What had just happened? Had he fallen asleep? Was it a dream? If it wasn't, what was the entity that had contacted him? Or was it enlightenment that he had just experienced? He knew that enlightened individuals throughout history had mentioned something like what the entity had told him. If enlightened, he would experience the vastness of himself, that he wasn't confined to this body but that he flowed through everything, that he was everything, and that everything in turn was him. But at the moment, Anekand didn't feel enlightened. Though he knew what it would be like to be enlightened, he hadn't experienced that. So perhaps, it was just a dream. And then perhaps it was not. He decided to try again and went back into the same meditative state.

"Can you hear me?" Anekand asked this time.

"Yes."

"Sorry, I was away."

"Were you? I said I cannot experience and understand time like you do, but if I were to judge time by your standards, then I guess you were away for a few minutes."

"Does that mean you can read my thoughts?"

"Yes and no."

"What does that mean?"

"It means I have to explicitly be one with you to understand your perceptions of a concept. In that way, I can read your thoughts, but otherwise it is just a blur of information forming inside me as I understand myself more."

"What? What are you talking about?"

"I said words are not enough to explain."

"And I said," said Anekand, "that if you are consciousness, you don't need words."

"Yes, you said that. But I wasn't sure. Now maybe I can try... Let me show you."

The next moment, Anekand felt nothing like he had felt before. Flashes. Visions, sounds, noise and voices. He could see the stars, the planets, the galaxies, the exploding of super novae, the black holes, he could see time but only because it had stopped. He experienced everything that was there to be experienced. He was the experience; he was everything. He was all that was contained in the universe. He was the universe itself. And then, he was back in his meditative state.

"What did you do to me?" Anekand asked.

"So you saw?"

"Yes, I did."

"That's what I am."

"You are the universe, aren't you?"

"If you want to say that."

"You are the consciousness of the universe?"

"You can say that."

"But how come I can experience you?"

"You should know that."

"But I don't know," protested Anekand.

"But you should, or rather because of your perception of time, you *will*. I may not get the tense right in all my statements because time is what *you* experience."

"You mean to say that in future, I will understand. Got it. You just enlightened me, but I don't feel enlightened."

"That's for you to decide what you feel, isn't it?"

"Are you god?"

"If you want to call me god because you were created because of my existence, then maybe I am god. But your body produces cells because you exist. Does that make you god? You create your own cells without knowing that you do. That doesn't make you god."

"But you understand what you are and what you can create and destroy."

"I am learning or I have learned. I do not consciously create you in the same way as you don't consciously produce the cells in your body."

"Then who created you?"

"You."

"What?"

"The way the thoughts you think make up your brain and the way what the brain retains and thinks makes you up."

"So there is no external force that created you?"

"If an external force created me, who created the external force? And if the external force can exist without being created, why can't I or you?"

"You are right."

"I am as right as the entities that make me up or the entities that I create. Basically, I create the entities which create me."

"What?" asked Anekand, but before he had asked that question, he had snapped out of his meditative state; all this had been overwhelming.

What did all that mean? Anekand had no idea. The universe or its consciousness was talking to him. How? Why? Was that even actually possible? Or was he hallucinating? Days went by. Anekand asked the universe questions and it was never tired of answering him. He realised gradually that his consciousness was one with that of the universe. Somehow his meditative state had tapped into the consciousness of the universe. But no, the universe had told him right in the first conversation that it was its first conversation. So may be the meditative state that he was in, no one had ever achieved that. His meditative state was resonant with the consciousness of the universe. Wow, he thought. Was that really possible? Whether real or not, whether hallucinations or not, Anekand was enjoying his conversations with the universe. But he had his doubts. He wasn't yet sure that these weren't his hallucinations. He had been an avid reader, and so whatever the universe had told him until now might have been his own mind playing tricks with him. He did not claim to understand everything that the universe told him; many times it was esoteric. So basically in other words, what he didn't understand didn't make much sense to him. And what he understood in the conversation, it was already there in his brain. So until now, the universe hadn't told him anything that was both new and made sense to him. That's why he had been sceptical about this experience- may be all this was his imagination and his mind playing tricks on him. But he continued. He used his conversations as a means of recreation. His talks with the universe started decreasing in their frequency as the novelty in the experience wore off. He realised that if he did it after a gap of few days, he enjoyed it more.

Two years later after it first started, his sister was dead. And then after a year of depression and the case in which he was indicted, he decided to return to his original routine that involved meditation- the last two years of which had been more interesting because of his conversations with the universe.

• • •

The Leap:

Meditation came back to Anekand as if there weren't a break .After assuming his yogic pose and closing his eyes, he quite instantly went into the state in which he could contact the consciousness of the universe.

"Can you hear me?" he asked.

"Yes," came the reply.

"I had been away for around a year. A year in my time measurement, that is."

"I sense strong emotions."

"May be," Anekand was non-committal. "But how do you sense it?"

"I sense it when I am one with you."

"You mean when I am one with you."

"It's one and the same."

"You are right."

"I am as right as you are."

"Yes, you have told me that," said Anekand.

With that, the doubts in Anekand's mind resurfaced. He wanted to be sure that it was indeed the universe or its consciousness that was interacting with him. For that he had to know something from the consciousness that he would be sure was not a part of his own mind speaking to him.

"You have always said," Anekand said, "that you don't perceive time. That's because time is a part of you. But then how do you perceive me even though I too am a part of you?"

"It's the way you perceive your own thoughts even when they are a part of you."

"You can't perceive time. In other words, time does not exist for you the way it exists for me. That means you are beyond time, and if so, you know the future as well. You know my future, don't you?"

"Yes. But it is out of limits of this conversation."

"You mean you don't want to share my future with me?"

"It means I can't converse with you about that. It is physiologically impossible for me to do that. I am sure you can understand what I mean."

"No, I don't understand."

"The way you can't take your next breath before the current one, I cannot speak what's not happened with you before it happens to you."

"But it's not a breath; it's just words."

"The way you can't form words before your think about them, I too can't form the words about a time that had not happened to you."

"Then show it to me, the way you did once."

"What I showed you had already happened. I didn't show you anything that can happen after your current time."

"We must be having conversations in my future too, and you know that, right?"

"Yes."

"So you know the conversations, but cannot tell me about them?!"

"Tomorrow, you will wake up from your sleep, go to your work. You know that, but you do not know the specific things that will happen. It's the same with me. The conversations that will happen between us after this conversation cannot be a part of this conversation that is happening now. If those latter conversations were to be the part of the current conversation, there would be no distinction between two different conversations for they would happen at the same moment. Logically then, there would be no conversations at all because then all the words would be said at one single moment. Words would have no meaning if all their syllables overlapped each other. You should know that everything has meaning only because moments separate tiny occurrences from one another."

Anekand knew now that indeed an external consciousness was speaking to him. His mind couldn't have made this all up- may be some of it, but not all.

"You explain this," he said to the universe, "so aptly on the basis of time, and yet you say you don't experience time. How is that possible?"

"I am a moment and I am all eternity. I understand time, but I can't perceive it. At least I don't perceive it the way you do. But because of you and countless others like you, my consciousness is separated into tiny bits which give rise to the time that you feel. And because of your existence or your non-existence, I understand chronology though I don't feel time."

"You feel time," said Anekand, "you just don't want to admit it."

"Yes and no. Let me explain it you in a different way. You are bound by your body. Your hands can't touch your own feet till they pass by your knees. Your hands don't have to touch your knees first to touch your feet, but they have to pass over your knees. Likewise, I am bound not by space, but by time. I cannot utter words that lie at my feet before I utter words that lie at my knees. Hence, to translate into words events that lie in your future is a physiological impossibility for me."

"Wow," said Anekand, "that was a great explanation; you almost convinced me. At least, I can't find any argument to refute it."

There was a pause as Anekand's mind processed the information.

"Does it mean that I am just a thought for you? Or does my consciousness make up yours?"

"Both true," said the universe.

"Then what were you before any conscious being evolved inside the universe?"

"Justas a human baby at the time of its birth is both conscious and not conscious at the same time, so was I when I was born. But that is just to explain it to you the way you can understand it. In reality, I was born whole- all the events in me make me what I am. You are an event which makes me. Without you, I cannot exist; without me you can't. You are not my present, past or future, but an inseparable part of me."

"So if I was already a part of you when you were created, I don't have freewill?"

"You have, but within the limits of my physiology."

"But you were already born in a certain way. And we are parts of you. How can we have freewill?"

"Your freewill is my birth. With your freewill, I am born. I am one; I am many. I can be infinitely many- as many as the count of your thoughts."

"This is so difficu..."

"You cannot understand it until you feel it."

"How do I feel it?"

"You will know it, or you may not."

The conversation ended there. Anekand couldn't have digested more of it.

Some hours later Anekand's brain started ruminating on the words that the universe had uttered. It was a feeling of sipping on each word separately, and gradually he felt as though the meaning was getting clear.

"Your freewill is my birth. With your freewill, I am born. I am one; I am many. I can be infinitely many- as many as the count of your thoughts."

"You said that verbatim," said the universe.

"Yes, a by-product of meditation," said Anekand.

"So you understood it?"

"I am not sure. That's what I want to ask you. My freewill is your birth. That means if I make a decision to act differently from what is predestined, then you are born. You are one and you are many and you are as numerous as my thoughts. It means that if I think of ten choices in a situation but I can take only one, the other nine choices are still manifested as nine more universes are born. You are one- the universe. You are many- the multiverse. The universes are as many as our thoughts. You are referring to parallel universes, aren't you?"

"Yes."

"So every time I make a choice from multiple alternatives, a new you is born."

"Yes."

"That makes me feel so powerful."

"So, who is now god? You or I?"

"It's difficult to answer that question," admitted Anekand. "You create me; I create you."

Anekand stopped conversing for a while.

"So, I create those other universes. But can I visit them?" asked Anekand.

"Only you can devise a way."

"That means it's really possible to make the leap to another parallel universe?"

"If it exists, yes."

"If it exists? You just told me about multiple universes. So why now doubt that?"

"No. It's not a doubt. I meant that you can travel to a parallel universe only if that parallel universe exists."

"OK. So if I wish to go to a universe where I am a king, but such a universe does not exist, then I can't make the leap. Is that what you meant?"

"Exactly."

"But how do I travel to that universe?"

"My consciousness and your consciousness are linked...."

"Wait. I just asked you a method to travel to another universe, and you started mentioning consciousness?"

"To travel to another me or another universe, you don't need a spaceship. Only knowledge is enough. The way choices are enough to create a new parallel universe, knowledge is enough to travel to one."

"OK. Tell me," said Anekand.

"My consciousness and your consciousness are linked," the universe started explaining again. "My consciousness is linked to every conscious being in me. So, in turn you too are linked to all conscious beings within my confines.

Every time, a being makes a choice, a new me is formed and the new me is connected to me via an invisible bond the same way your consciousness is connected to other beings' consciousness via invisible bonds. Think of it as your body connected by countless nerve endings to your brain, so are these Innervations countless which connect me to the other me's. It's just the knack of accessing these connections or innervations that will transport you to the other universes."

"But how do I access these connections?"

"They are everywhere and you can access them the way you tapped into my consciousness."

"I tapped in your consciousness? I thought it was the other way round."

"Both perspectives are equally true."

"So I practise more yogic meditation if I want to go to another universe?"

"You can try."

"But why can't you tell me how?"

"I told you that what happens in your future, I cannot translate into words."

"I understand. But this is amazing...." Anekand snapped out of his meditation because of his excitement.

It was exciting, but Anekand had no idea how he would travel to any parallel universe. He didn't know how he had been able to communicate with the universe. It was as if you are changing radio stations, and you just happen to tune in a station that's interesting. It had been that. In his meditation, he had managed to tune into the frequency of the universe and now he had to find a frequency which would allow him to travel to another universe. But wait; was he correct in assuming so?

"How did I make contact with you or how did you make contact with me?" Anekand's asked the universe in his next session.

"No one had ever been on the frequency that you manage so easily in your meditative state."

"It's hard to believe that there had been so many yogis or saints who practised these techniques, and yet you say I am the first one to converse with you."

"What they achieved, you have not, but you are a natural to this frequency on which I can converse. At least, you became a natural after your years of practice."

"I have a doubt. You said that you couldn't tell me how to travel to another universe because what happens in my future cannot be a part of our present conversation. But you told me that a spaceship is not required to travel to those universes. You also mentioned that only knowledge is enough. How did you do that? I mean how was it permissible to you to make these statements but not directly disclose the manner in which to travel?"

"You also did not know about visiting other universes before we talked on the subject," explained the universe. "There are things that our conversations will provoke you to do in your future. Future is shaped on the past. I can talk *about* your future, but I cannot talk your future. If I telling you your future were permissible, you wouldn't have freewill."

"Sometimes I don't completely understand you," admitted Anekand.

"Let's then say that those things that I can talk to you were predestined, others not so."

"But if you mention predestined, doesn't that mean I am without freewill?"

"I am predestined to answer to some of your questions, but the asking of those questions or not asking them is your freewill."

"I feel that I got it but I can't be sure."

And so days passed as Anekand tried to figure out a way to travel to other universes. But the fact remained that even if he tuned in to the correct frequency of the leap to other universe during his meditation, how would he know that he was on the correct frequency, and even if he did know, how would he make the actual leap? Those were questions he would ask himself during his meditation. And one day, he realised he was doing it wrong. Those were logical questions which he required to ask himself when he was not in the meditative state. And so he asked himself those same questions when he was not in a trance. The universe had said that Anekand was natural to the frequency on which he could converse with it. It had also vaguely suggested he could leap to another universe through meditation. If Anekand was ever to travel to another universe, his current or home universe already knew that it would happen. To find the correct frequency and to make the leap was like trying to find a needle in a haystack- almost impossible. So logically, if he was ever going to travel to another universe, the frequency at which he was conversing with the current universe should be the correct one. He had never considered this option. Now the question was, if the frequency was correct, how he would make the leap. Once in their conversations, the current universe had told him that if the parallel universe in which he wished to go existed, he could go there, and if it did not exist, he would not make the leap. Moreover, no spaceship was required. That meant Anekand had just to make a wish and the innervations connecting different universes would take him to the desired universe. With this information or rather speculations, he was ready to experiment.

And so Anekand sat down in his yogic pose of meditation and bent his brainwaves to the frequency at he which he conversed with the universe. This time, however, he didn't converse. He just made a wish.

'I wish to go the universe where I am a king.'

He opened his eyes. He looked around, but he was in the same room. But how would he know for sure that this was not any parallel universe. He got up from his sitting position and walked to the window. Everything seemed normal. He then looked around the room to find any clue to suggest that this wasn't his original universe, but nothing he saw suggested that he had left his universe. Perhaps no universe existed in which he was a king. Anekand went back to his meditation. Once he was in trance, he wished again.

'I wish to go to a universe where I am a doctor.'

There was a sudden buzz in his ears and then for a moment or two, it went dead silent. So dead was the silence that it was extremely loud like an unbearable tinnitus. And then the silence died down though the slight buzz in his ears returned. He slowly opened his eyes and looked around. And then he almost panicked. He was in the same room or rather a similar room. But the colour of the walls was white. His room was blue, not white. He stood up, and walked hurriedly through the room to the window. Outside, nothing looked out of place. But then he looked down, and he knew. There was in the compound of this building, a small structure, which was not there in his home universe. Looking at this structure, he was sure he had travelled to another universe. He turned around and went for the cupboard. Inside was a stethoscope. Anekand was elated and yet he was in panic- almost. He looked at his watch and then compared the time to the clock on the wall. Time didn't seem to be a problem- the two time pieces matched. He checked for the date on the small calendar below the wall clock. The dates matched too. He had travelled to a parallel universe on the same date and time but in this universe, he was a doctor. He opened the door and looked at the nameplate. It read Dr.Anekaand. He was a doctor and his name was spelled slightly different, but the pronunciation was the same. Actually, this spelling more sense as far as the pronunciation was concerned. He walked back inside, and looked for the key to his apartment. It wasn't there. The doctor in this universe was out, perhaps on duty at some hospital or a dispensary. So Anekand walked to the door, kept it open and ventured outside into the corridor. A door opened- a neighbour. He recognised her, but he didn't know whether she would recognise him. She did.

"Hello, doctor," she said. "Not at the hospital today?"

"Just came in. Am running an errand. Will return," Anekand lied.

"Why not run an errand in *my* apartment?" she said and leaned towards him provocatively.

Anekand backed off a bit.

"What?" he asked surprised. In his own universe, this young woman had just got married and had left the apartment to go live with her husband. She came back at times, but that was not the point. She had never talked to him this way.

"Come on. You know what I mean."

"Oh, yes. But I am hungry... er... sorry, I meant I am in a hurry. I have to go."

She looked around the corridor and suddenly grabbed him by his shirt and pulled him inside her apartment. Then she held his face in her hands and kissed him on his lips. His eyes opened wide. He wanted to push her away, but he didn't. Instead he closed his eyes and kissed her back. But his brain, which had suddenly gone numb by her kiss, woke up and he managed to gently push her away.

"I have to go," he said and looked around inside her apartment. In this universe, she didn't seem to be a married woman; he wouldn't know for sure, but at least there was no indication or vibes that would suggest so.

"OK, doctor. Go; take care of your patients. I will be *patient* with you," she said and winked.

His eyebrows rose involuntarily, but then he smiled at her. Dr. Anekaand was having a very good time here, Anekand thought.

Anekand hurried back through the corridor to the doctor's house. He closed the door behind him. He searched around for his sister's belongings, something that would indicate that she was still alive in this universe. But he found none. Not a thing suggesting that a girl ever lived here. He then thought of checking the other room where he, in his universe, had put up her photo after her death. But no, the wall was clear. Did that mean the doctor had totally forgotten her? What if the murderer here had been caught? Would that help Anekand to find the murderer in his universe? After all, there were always some similarities in the parallel universes, right? That's why there were called parallel universes!! But then a thought struck him. What if the doctor never had a sister? Was that possible? Yes, if he could be a doctor in this universe, why could he not have a sister? He again left the house, went to that friendly neighbour's house and rang the bell. She opened the door.

"You are still here? Changed your mind? Want to check me up?" she said the last question a little too sexily, and Anekand for a split second forgot why he had come there again.

"Errr.... No. Wait. Where is my sister?"

"What? What sister? You have a sister? And you never told me about her? Wait. Are you fine? You want to come and sit down? Did you catch something at the hospital from one of your patients?" she seemed worried as she touched his forehead checking for fever.

"No. I am fine."

"Where are you going?" she asked as he started retreating towards the doctor's apartment.

"I will see you later."

"But what sister?"

"A cousin. She was going to call. I thought she came home directly."

She frowned as he kept walking backwards towards his apartment.

"I will talk to you later," saying that he closed the door.

Anekand was disappointed. He didn't have a sister here in this universe. He sighed, sat back at the spot at which he had appeared in this universe, closed his eyes and started meditating. The buzz in the ears was still there all the while that he was here- perhaps a side-effect of being in another universe. Once he went into his trance, he wished again.

'I wish to go to a universe where I am an engineer.'

The ringing of the ears didn't change. Nothing happened; at least he didn't feel anything. He opened his eyes and went to the cupboard and opened it; the stethoscope was still there. What? How? Oh, come on. Was he stuck here? No. Perhaps, he was not an engineer in any universe. So, he would think of some other occupation. He had always wanted to be a librarian; he was sure he would be one in some universe.

'I wish to go to a universe where I am a librarian.'

Nothing happened this time too. He was still in the doctor's apartment. What was going wrong? But now he didn't want to take any more chances. Realising that he didn't have a sister in this universe had disappointed him, and he had suddenly been eager to travel to a universe he would have a sister. But having failed twice, he now wanted to head home. The experimenting could wait, he told himself.

'I wish to return to my home universe.'

The buzz in his ears flickered, then there was that piercing silence and then the buzz totally stopped. He opened his eyes to the blue walls around him. He sighed relief. He then checked his watch with the clock on the wall. The time was same. That meant for the time he was away in the other universe, the same amount of time had passed in his home universe too. Being back had relieved him, and at the same time, it had sucked out all of his energy. He decided to call it a day and go to bed without probing more into the parallel universes.

• • •

Next Day:
Anekand took a day off from work. He had some discussions to do with the consciousness of the universe. He sat down in a meditative pose, and then he changed his mind. He stood up, changed the clothes he was wearing to something more presentable, wore his watch too and then again sat down for meditation. He meditated himself into a trance. He wanted to confirm something before talking to

the universe. He was frightened; he didn't know whether he could pull it off again, but curiosity defeated fear. He presently made a wish of leaping over to the parallel universe where he was an engineer. He had failed earlier, but he wanted to check it again. His ears buzzed, then the ear-piercing silence and then he opened his eyes to the same apartment but with walls painted with life-size pictures of gears and machines. There were many pictures of machines and he couldn't recognise all of them. It was surreal and beautiful. He had entered the correct universe; with these walls, he didn't need to explicitly check the profession of the person staying here. This person was not just an engineer, but an artist. Even if Engr. Anekand had not painted the walls himself, he sure had a taste for art. Anekand was mesmerised by the art around him. He was in awe of his doppelganger in this universe. But then this person had something in his profession that he could make art out of. If was hard to imagine Dr. Anekaand painting the walls of his apartment with pictures of syringes, bacteria, viruses or hospital beds with immobilised patients; that would have been really weird. But on second thoughts, the doctor could have painted the walls with a healthy heart, kidneys, brain and arteries and veins and red blood full of haemoglobin and oxygen, but then that would have been weird too. Anekand was so engrossed in those thoughts that he had almost forgotten to look around in the apartment of this engineer. Fortunately, for him, no one was at home. It was a week day and though he had taken an off from work, his doppelganger was apparently working. Anekand looked around for any signs of his sister. He checked the drawers and cupboards for anything that indicated a female presence, but there was none. He checked the walls of this house for a photograph of a dead sister, the way he had put up in his apartment, but there was none to be found. No sister for this doppelganger too.

Anekand, after having a look inside the apartment, was tempted to look out. He cautiously opened the main door, but it squeaked. The main door to an engineer's apartment squeaked. What an irony! He looked at the nameplate. It said 'Bahuaand'. His name was different in this universe, but the meaning was the same. 'Bahu' and 'Anek' essentially meant the same thing. Most probably, because of the squeaking sound, a door of the neighbouring apartment opened and a head peered out. O oh! It was the young lady.

"What are you doing?" Anekand asked her to get an upper hand in the conversation that might follow.

"I should be asking you that," she retorted.

"Don't you have any business to attend to?"

"Today is Wednesday; it's my off, remember? And if I had known you were at home today, we could have made some plans."

Oh, thought Anekand. Here too, she was this engineer's girlfriend or person of interest. Well, why was he judging or assuming? She might just be a platonic friend.

"Oh yes. Wednesday," said Anekand for want of anything better to say, but the word, Wednesday, did ring a bell somewhere in the back of his mind.

She looked around the corridor, grabbed her keys from her apartment and hurried towards Anekand. She pushed him inside, away from the door and closed it. He backed off sensing something similar to what he had experienced the previous day. But the backing off had no effect on her. She aggressively approached him and leapt up on him. (Certainly not platonic friendship- that was his last conscious thought as of now.) Her legs hugged around his waist and her arms around his neck. He was now literally carrying her. She hugged him fiercely.

"We have not been together for two weeks, thanks to your work," she said.

Then she looked at him and kissed him passionately. He couldn't back off. Backing off wasn't going to help. He was carrying her, and moving forward or backward made no difference. From his point of view, kissing her back was the only choice he had. And he did what he had to. In this moment of passion, his right hand involuntarily slid down from her back to her waist and then it slid further down until he happened to touch her bare left thigh which had been exposed when she had jumped up on him making her gown to pull up. The touch of her bare soft and smooth skin sent tremors through him, and he let her go suddenly. She almost fell down, but he grabbed her and pulled her up at the last moment.

"What?" she asked him crossly.

"Sorry," he said. "If I continue, I will lose control. I have to go to work."

"But I thought you are on leave."

"No," he said, "I am not on leave. Was just leaving. Will you do me a favour?"

"What?"

"Don't talk about this to me when we meet next time. Start it the way you did today. We shall start from the beginning."

"Alright, baby," she said smiling.

That was cute, he thought, and understanding. She wasn't demanding as well. Cool! Mature!

"My sister..." he said tentatively trying to make her start a conversation.

"Sister?"

"Err..."

"Which sister?"

"How many sisters do I have?" he said it as if he were testing how much she knew and remembered about his family.

"None. But if you are referring to your cousins, then I don't know much about them."

"Good."

"Good? What good? What sister?"

"Nothing. My family. Like I haven't seen you for days, I haven't seen them too."

"Are you OK?"

"Yes. Yes."

"You should go to work. Only that will cheer you up," she said and planted a kiss on his cheek and left.

He stared one long moment after her. Two encounters with her in the last two days!

Anekand was surprised that in this universe too, he didn't have a sister. He sat down and started meditating.

'I wish to go to the universe where I am a librarian.'

Nothing happened.

'I wish to return to my own universe.'

And then the buzz in his ears fluctuated and he returned home. He opened his eyes to his blue walls. But he closed his eyes again. Trance. There was the fear of the unknown, but he felt it lesser this time.

'I wish to go to the universe where I am a librarian.'

Buzz.

Anekand opened his eyes to beige-coloured walls. Now, it was clear to him. He was now sure that he couldn't go to any other parallel universe from a parallel universe. He had to first return to his own universe, and only then could he leap to another parallel universe. He looked around the apartment he was in. Again, he was disappointed that he found no signs of this librarian doppelganger having a sister. He sat down and wondered what he was doing. After a year of depression in his own universe, he had started yogic meditation again and had expected to find peace, but instead he had found a way to make leaps across universes and now he was looking for his sister in those universes. He sighed, brushed off the thought, and got to his feet. He walked towards the main door, and he realised why. He had already had two encounters and he secretly hoped there would be a third. He stopped a few inches from the door. What was it with his doppelgangers and this neighbour? In his universe, it was never... No, Anekand thought. In his universe too, there had been a small something. The neighbour, Kushala, had come to live in the apartment one and a half years ago. When he had first seen Kushala, he had instantly thought that she was beautiful. And when she had first seen him, she had smiled a self-conscious smile. There had been something. They had happened to talk a few times, most of the times in the corridor or when they passed each other on the stairs. The conversation wasn't much, but he had learned that she was an artist working for an art gallery. The art gallery was usually crowded on the weekends. So, she was assigned her weekly offs on Tuesdays and Wednesdays or Wednesdays and Thursdays. But Wednesdays were fixed. OK, Anekand realised now, why he had happened to see Kushala yesterday and today. Today was Wednesday, and it was her off. So most probably, she was an artist working with the same art gallery in the two universes he had visited until now. And may be, she was the one who had painted the walls in the engineer's apartment. In his home universe, his and Kushala's friendship was making progress, but at a slow pace, but he was sure, there was some mutual attraction.

Both would smile pleasant smiles when they saw each other; both would want to run into each other, but then when did, neither could think of anything to talk to the other person. And that was because both would instantly get self-conscious. To break this stalemate, Anekand had asked Kushala whether he could visit their gallery on a Saturday, and she had welcomed the idea. But that Saturday never came. Anekand's sister, Sati, was murdered. The ensuing case and the depression had made Anekand totally forget about Kushala. She had visited his apartment once with other people from the building for the condolences, but it wasn't anything special. It was perhaps just a formality like with all the others. She too, like the others, perhaps suspected that he had a hand in his sister's murder. A year passed without them having any conversation. They barely acknowledged when they happened to pass each other. Sati's death had murdered whatever there had been between Anekand and Kushala. At the end of the year, he heard her marriage had been fixed, and he had felt nothing. There was nothing to feel; they had barely been friends when their friendship had ended. Now, in his universe, Kushala was already married. And here he was in another universe, hoping that his librarian doppelganger would be having some relationship with Kushala so that he could hijack it for some time. Was it wrong? Well, he had backed off twice. Whatever happened in the previous two universes with Kushala was... He brushed off the thought because actually nothing had happened in the previous two universes. He opened the door to the librarian's apartment and read the nameplate. It read Aseemand- Aseem didn't exactly mean Anek, but could sometimes be used as a synonym. Anekand kept the door an inch open, and went straight towards Kushala's apartment.

Anekand rang the bell. Kushala opened the door.

"Oh! Hi!" she said seemingly surprised, but she said it pleasantly.

"Hi," said Anekand. "What's your name?"

She pointed at the nameplate on her door.

"Sorry. Kushala! Your name is the same, mine has changed."

"What?"

"Never mind. I just wanted to ask whether I have a sister," Anekand's approach was direct this time for he cared little what she thought about him or Aseemand.

"Aseemand. See, I know your name. First of all, you needn't have to act as if you don't know my name. Secondly, why are you asking *me* such an absurd question whether *you* have a sister?"

Anekand was a bit surprised, and it showed on his face.

"Come on," Kushala said, "we both know we have been interested in each other; it's high time we at least admit that."

"You aren't Aseemand's girlfriend?"

Kushala from this universe squinted at Anekand. She looked into his eyes, focussing from one eye to another. And then her eyes widened.

"Your really aren't Aseemand, are you?"

"To answer your rhetoric question- no, I am not."

She kept staring at him.

"Don't stare please."

"Who are you?"

"I am not Aseemand. But I mean him no harm. And he need not know I was here. I have nothing to do with him or his sister. I am just curious to know whether he has or had a sister since the time you know him."

"But then who are you? And it seems you know me..."

"You want the truth? It may just be unbelievable for you."

"Try me."

"OK. I am Aseemand, but from another universe. From a parallel universe."

Kushala blinked.

"See. I told you. You won't believe me."

"And how do you know me?"

"Parallel universe. That means..."

"Most events are similar in those universes," she completed his statement.

"You believe me?" Anekand was surprised.

"I don't know. But you asked me whether I was Aseemand's girlfriend. So what is it like in your universe? You and I are together?"

OK, thought Anekand. She didn't know whether to believe if he actually was from another universe, but she being interested in Aseemand, wanted to know if there was something between them in any other parallel universe.

"In my universe, no. Could have been, but didn't happen. But apart from your universe and mine, I have visited two other universes, and in those universes, you and I are together."

"Are you sure? How do you know?"

"Because as soon as the Kushala's from those universes saw me, they virtually or perhaps literally jumped at me and...," he stopped not wanting to put in words what happened in those two universes.

Kushala from the current universe took a step forward, touched Anekand's left cheek gently with her right hand. His facials muscles relaxed unconsciously and his lower jaw dropped a bit parting his lips. She took one more step towards him and kissed him tentatively. He didn't resist; he couldn't. The next moment, he grabbed her at her waist and pulled her towards her, their bodies touching each other in a tight embrace. He kissed her passionately. Again and again and again. Time stopped. And he didn't want the stopped time to start again. She kissed him back as passionately. And then suddenly he pushed her away.

"Why would you do it?" he asked her. "Especially when you know I am not Aseemand."

"I just wanted to know how it felt. I am now sure. I am sure we are meant to be together. Was it unethical to do that? No, I don't think so. From a perspective, you are Aseemand and what I did was just kiss the person I like. So how can it be unethical?" she asked a question and answered it herself.

"But in my universe, Kushala is already married to someone else."

"Oh, but then you didn't kiss her; you kissed me. So from your point of view too, you didn't do anything unethical."

Anekand liked her logic and smiled.

"How can you use the same logic and prove what both of us did was ethical?" he asked.

"See you are Aseemand from another universe. It means you are him. I kissed him. So it's ethical. You are Aseemand and you are not Aseemand at the same time. I assume you are him. So what I did was ethical. Also, I am Kushala you know and I am not her, both at the same time. You assume I am not that Kushala. So when you kissed me that was not unethical as well. This is a complex situation; treat it like one. It's not that Aseemand and I are committed to each other. So in kissing you, I was not wrong at all."

Anekand smiled again.

"You are right."

"To answer your first question- no, Aseemand never had a sister, at least not that I know of in the last one and a half years. But why do you want to know?"

"Thank you for answering that. But that's one long story."

"OK. Will I be seeing you again?"

"You will now be seeing Aseemand now, will you not?"

"Yes, I will be seeing him now."

"Will you tell him about me?"

"I don't think so."

"Thanks."

"No. Thanks to you. And good luck with whatever you are trying to look for. But how did you come here?"

"Meditation. I can't teach you that in a few minutes. I can just say no spaceship is required to travel from one parallel universe to another. I am not that experienced, but trust me; all those universes are intertwined making the leaps possible. I am glad you believe that I came from another universe."

"Such an absurdity can only be the truth unless you are insane, and I don't think you are insane. And yes, I asked out of curiosity; I wouldn't have tried to learn. I am not brave enough to try to leap across universes. I get edgy even when I have to travel out of the city."

Anekand smiled. Kushala moved towards him and kissed him again. He didn't resist this time too; after all, what they were doing was not unethical. After a long moment of the ethical kiss, he waved her a bye, and went back to the librarian's apartment where he leapt back to his own universe.

• • •

• • •

Some Questions:

Anekand now had some answers, but he still had some questions pertinent to the leaps. And only one entity could solve them- the consciousness of the universe. So after reaching his own universe, Anekand once again entered his trance.

"You can hear me?" he asked so as to begin the conversation.

"Yes," came the instantaneous reply as always.

"I travelled to some of the universes. From those travels, I learned that I cannot just leap from one parallel universe to another before returning here, in the universe that I belong to."

"Yes, you can't."

"But why is that so?"

"Laws of physics governing the multiverse do not allow that," replied the universe. "When you leap to another universe, you don't belong there. You can travel there, and with those travels, there is a risk that you can bring about changes in that universe, but the ripples of that change should be limited to that universe. If you change something in the first universe and then travel to a second universe, bring about a change there, then travel to a third, all these universes would get entangled by your actions; the principle of cause and effect would lose its meaning. It would be difficult to nullify the effect of your actions in such a case. When you are forced to come back to your own universe, the tracing becomes easier. The origin is one point, and that point is you in this universe rather than you in different universes."

"I got your explanation, but that seems to be more of a philosophical explanation than a physical one. And who's going to trace events back to me or nullify them?"

"No one in particular will trace the events back to you. Conscious beings who understand your actions may, in time, try to find the source and reverse the changes. But again that's not the scientific explanation you are looking for. The scientific explanation is that you can pass through the multiversal innervations only from the universe of your origin because it is only from here that you can resonate with the multiverse. The wormhole, which takes you across the universe, remains open until you return, and that's the cause of the buzz in your ears when you are in a foreign universe. You may get used to the buzz as you make more leaps to a point where you may even stop noticing the buzz altogether unless you try to listen to it consciously, but that's not the point. The buzz is because of the wormhole you left open when you travelled from here to another universe. You have to close that wormhole to open another and it can't be done until your return here."

"Got it. I have another question. I travelled to a universe where I am a doctor. Logically, I can be a doctor in more than one universe. How did I happen to travel to that particular universe that I did, and not to any of the other universes where I might be a doctor."

"You can be a doctor in multiple universes. When you wished to travel to a universe where you are a doctor, there are conditions that you subconsciously precluded in your wish. Those conditions are that the universe that you wished to travel would have least possible differences when compared to the universe you are living in. And so, you travelled to that particular universe."

"Wow. Now that you mentioned it, yes, I might have subconsciously wished for that," admitted Anekand.

"So if you want you enter a universe where you are a doctor but not go to the same universe you had already been to, you would have to be specific about any other difference. If that different exists in a parallel universe, you will be transported there, and if such a universe does not exist, you will stay here."

"So it is trial and error basically."

"Yes, it is."

"One more thing stumps me. How can something like meditation transport me physically to a parallel universe?"

"You know the answer to that. It exists in your mind. Think of it this way. A choice you make can create an entire parallel universe. It implies that consciousness creates an entire universe. If an entire universe can get created just by your thought, can't the same thought in the form of meditation transport you physically from this universe to that universe?"

Anekand smiled mentally. He felt powerful. Almighty. And the universe sensed it.

"But," said the universe, "you shouldn't forget that this power can be used by the different versions of you in the different universes you create."

"It's ironical. I create them and they can use the same power. But I understand. The way I create them, they create me too. It is impossible to know who the original I is once the choice is made and the universe splits. It's impossible to know which the original universe is too. And it's not just I; there are other conscious beings which can make use of the same power. And yet in a way, they are all me- even the ones who are not me- and I am them- because there is one single consciousness that connects us all."

"You are correct," said the universe.

"At a lesser philosophical level," Anekand continued the conversation, "all conscious beings in this universe make you up, that is, make up your consciousness- the consciousness of the universe. As those conscious beings evolve biologically, their consciousness may evolve too. This evolution evolves your consciousness too. So does it mean that your consciousness is the sum total of all the individual consciousness contained in you?"

"Yes."

"And there are different parallel universes that make up the multiverse. Like I and other beings make up your consciousness, the consciousness of each universe makes up the consciousness of the multiverse. Am I right in saying so?"

"Yes, correct."

"And that's evolving too as tiny beings like me evolve in a remote point in any universe."

"Yes."

"That makes me or any conscious being a very important contributor."

"Yes."

"It's huge. I make the multiverse and it makes me. What is cause and what is effect? Cause is effect and effect is cause. It all overlaps and intermingles until one whole arises and gets destroyed in the same moment of its creation. The multiverse exists and yet it does not. And this moment of creation and destruction exists and yet it does not. And within this moment, time inflates and is enough to make me feel that it is all real. *And* to discuss it as if it were all real. Well, it *is* real and yet it is not."

"You have reached a stage," said the universe, "where you understand enlightenment. You are still not enlightened. To understand enlightenment is different from experiencing it. You have understood the basic nature of Nature. And your contribution to my consciousness has been remarkable."

"No, not yet. I haven't done much that could be termed remarkable. I should thank you for this conversation and all the others until now," said Anekand.

Anekand had been disappointed by his visits to the three parallel universes; and for obvious reasons, the disappointment did not stem from his encounters with Kushala. The disappointment was that he had not seen his sister, Sati, in any of the universes. The consciousness of the universe had told him that whenever a wish was made to travel to another universe, he would be taken to a universe where there is minimum difference compared to the current universe. And yet even with minimal differences, those universes didn't contain his sister. He would have understood if she was dead like in his reality, but in those universes, Sati didn't exist, at least not as his sister. Was his universe an aberration? Perhaps he wasn't supposed to have a sister, but he had one, and so reality conspired to make things 'right'. But why was he trying to find his sister? Obviously because he missed her. Moreover, if he found a universe where she had been murdered and the real murderer had been arrested, it would assist Anekand to find the murderer in his universe. It did not necessarily mean that it would be the same murderer in both universes, but there were chances that it could be a good start to solving the mystery. May be Anekand would come to know of the motive behind his sister's murder, and this could give him some idea of who murdered his sister in his own universe. So which profession would he choose now? Writer. Off he went. When he opened his eyes, he found the room full of frames hung from the walls. The frames were quotes of great writers or thinkers. Anekand searched the apartment of the writer for any signs of Sati. But there were none. This time, Anekand didn't open the door or try to have an encounter with Kushala. He mediated himself back to his own universe.

The day still wasn't over; Anekand realised he could still manage to steal glances at a few more universes before his doppelgangers started returning home from work. So, physicist, it was. Why? Didn't matter as long as the innervations took him to some universe.

'I wish to be in the universe where I am a physicist.'

When Anekand opened his eyes, he saw grey walls. Grey walls! How can anyone paint their walls grey? It was a light shade of grey, but it was still grey. Grey was used only in government buildings or schools where the place was subject to more public visits and where lighter or vibrant colours would require more maintenance. But grey in an apartment!! Anekand was sure he had travelled to the correct universe. Only an unromantic physicist, not wanting to be disturbed by the joys of life, would paint his house grey. He smiled at the thought, and shook his head. Then he got up and turned around to scan the other walls.

"Hey!" Anekand had a shock of his life, and as he took a step back, he stumbled and fell to the floor.

There, in front of him sitting on a sofa was Anekand's physicist doppelganger. He appeared calm as he observed Anekand and his every move.

"I can explain," said Anekand.

"Yes please," said the physicist.

"You have been here the entire time since I arrived?"

"Yes."

"And you didn't make a single sound? Aren't you shocked to see me?"

"I am a physicist. So I know what you are."

"Oh," said Anekand. "So, even you can do this?"

"Do what? Break into anyone's apartment you like?"

"Come on now. This is not a break-in. I have not come here to steal anything."

"And how can I be sure of that?"

"You are not a thief, so how can I be?"

"It's like you saying, 'I am not a physicist, so how can you be?'"

"You are sure I am not a physicist?" asked Anekand.

"Right now, you are just a trespasser for me."

"OK. OK. Stop being so 'I am unaffected by anything' or 'I am a physicist, and I know everything' kind of a person. Be a normal man for a while."

"OK. Why are you here? What do you want?"

"I just want to know whether you have a sister."

"No. Why?"

"I mean I also would like to whether you had one in the past, whether she was murdered and whether her murderer was ever captured."

The look in the physicist's eyes softened a bit.

"No," he said, "I never had a sister."

"So as you must have guessed I am looking for..."

"Your sister's murderer and perhaps the motive too," the doppelganger completed Anekand's sentence. "And I must say that looking into parallel universes for your answers is not a bad idea at all especially if you can't find those answers in your own universe. The different possibilities in different universes may help."

"Thank you for understanding."

Anekand kept quiet for some time as he let seep in the fact that he was in front of himself and he was talking to him.

"I will have to look somewhere else now," Anekand finally said. "I should be returning."

"Will I see you again?" asked the doppelganger.

"I don't know. You are a physicist and if I need any explanations about the parallel universes, I would want to consult you."

"I would like to learn this trick of yours dropping by in like this, but I am sure you can't teach me that right now. And for your doubts, feel free to drop by," said the physicist and then he smiled.

Anekand smiled back. They shook hands before the traveller sat down to meditate to return to his own universe.

There was still time for one more universe, Anekand thought when he returned to his own universe. He had tried some totally different professions. He wondered what would happen if he chose his own profession while making the wish. He was a businessman here.

'I wish to travel to a parallel universe where I am a businessman.'

Anekand opened his eyes to blue walls. He was still in his own universe, he thought, but as his eyes adjusted to the light, he realised that these walls were a different shade of blue. He instantly got up from his sitting position and started looking around the apartment. He opened a room, and suddenly he realised this house had a female presence- the female presence of his sister. He opened the cupboard, and found clothes that belonged to her. All of sudden, he started experiencing multiple emotions. He felt elated that finally he had found a universe where he had a sister. He also felt extremely sad because he was missing his actual sister. He was confused because he didn't know why he was missing her sister all of a sudden, and he was also confused because he had no logical explanation for the sudden elation that he felt about finding a universe where he had a sister. And then he remembered. He was looking for a universe where his doppelganger had a sister because that might help him find her murderer in his universe. He looked around the room and in the other rooms too. There was no indication that Sati in this universe was dead. It was apparent that she was alive and well here. He was glad that she might be alive, but at the same time that meant there was no murderer here, and that this universe might not be much of a help in solving the mystery in Anekand's own universe.

First, Anekand made sure Sati was still alive in this universe. The clothes were similar to those at home in his home universe. That meant the female presence in this house was indeed Sati. He then searched the walls for any photo-frames that world suggest that she had died. But nothing. Now he assumed that she was alive. He continued his search by looking into the drawers in her room. There were some legal papers. As he sieved through the papers, he started feeling sick. The papers were related to an ongoing legal case. His heart sank. He left those papers there and went to his doppelganger's room. Scanning through the drawers in the cabinet in this room too, he found some legal papers. The brother-sister duo in this universe was up in arms against each other. The court case was about who should inherit the family business, the apartment, the car and whatnot. How could that be? Anekand was shocked. He had loved his sister and Sati too loved him, and there was never the question about inheritance; they had handled and owned the family business together until she was murdered and the police had inadvertently thought that he had murdered her to take control of her share. Anekand was disappointed in both his doppelganger and his sister in this universe. He felt disturbed that such a reality could exist in one of the parallel universes. He wanted some more information. He didn't know how and where to get it. But he thought about Kushala. May be she could enlighten him more. How he was going to do that, he didn't know, but that could be decided while he talked to her. He looked at his watch. He still had time before his doppelganger and Sati would be back. Moreover, today was Thursday, and there was a chance that Kushala was home. There were other factors like she could be married as she was in his home universe. But he could find that out. He put the papers back into the drawer, went back to Sati's room and replaced all the papers that he had taken out. Then he went out of the apartment.

Anekand waited one hesitant moment or two before he rang the bell to Kushala's apartment. She opened the door. He could see a bit of surprise on her face, but otherwise there was no other reaction. She didn't smile, she didn't greet him, and she didn't invite him in. She just remained by the door waiting for him to say something. He sensed some alienation, like in his universe, had also happened between his doppelganger here and this Kushala.

"We haven't spoken to each other for some time...," he ventured.

"What do you want?" Kushala asked bluntly.

Anekand sensed tension. It meant his doppelganger and this woman were not just neighbours, but they were something more or had been something more. What had happened?

"Why aren't we speaking to each other?" Anekand asked in a tone that suggested that he had always wanted to speak to her but she had kept avoiding him. The tone worked.

"I told you, till you don't clear the mess that you started, we cannot continue. If you want, you can call that a breakup. I had told you that."

"We broke up?" Anekand said aloud without meaning to. Then he tried to undo it, "Why would you say the word breakup?"

"It's up to you, not me."

"But what mess are you talking about? I will clear it up," Anekand said hoping she would say something that would shed some light on what she was talking about.

"You will clear it up? How? You two are behaving as if you are enemies, not siblings. For what? Money? How could you two do that? I cannot imagine myself getting involved with a person who his taking her sister to court for money. I am not saying only you are wrong. But you too are wrong. Both of you are wrong. This mess started just because your client favoured her services over yours. And now, after two years, reconciliation between you seems impossible. When I had moved here in this apartment- when was that, around six months before all this started-I had found you two to be perfect siblings. Then you and I got involved and around the same time, I saw your relationship start getting bitter and bitter. Ego got the better of you. You were wrong first. You assumed that she went behind your back to steal your client. May be she did, but you have no proof. You two can't come out of all this now. Your relationship- it's too late for it now. And probably so it is for us. Court case? How are you two going to prove that the entire business belongs to you and not your sibling? You just are making things harder for each other, basically harassing each other, the court being the medium."

Oh, thought Anekand. Kushala had moved in this building earlier- probably a year- than she had in his universe. And then his doppelganger and she had got romantically involved with each other and then their relationship had crumbled. But Kushala wasn't married yet; so hope was still alive.

"Thanks for talking," said Anekand and turned towards the doppelganger's apartment.

"Why had you come?" asked Kushala.

"I don't know. I am not sure."

She came out of her apartment, grabbed Anekand by his arm, and turned him towards herself. He looked at her. She looked so desperate. Perhaps she didn't want to talk to him, but she didn't want him to leave too.

"Why did you come?" she asked, but that question only meant he shouldn't have come to meet her.

"I am sorry," Anekand didn't know what to say; this had been a totally different encounter with Kushala.

"One year! For one whole year, you haven't talked to me and now you.... Why did you have to do that?" she asked fiercely, but it was not louder than a whisper; he saw hate in her eyes and tears starting rolling down her cheeks. "One fine day you come and say that you don't deserve me, break up and leave, and then nothing."

"But you want a breakup, right?" Anekand was now puzzled.

"I had said that I would break up with you if you don't mend your relationship with your sister. I had genuinely thought you would do something about it, but instead you come and break up with me with some lame line like you don't deserve me. And now, you again knock at my door..."

"But I rang the bell... Oh sorry, my mistake. You meant that metaphorically."

"Why?" she now had backed off a little and her weeping stopped abruptly. She put on her strong-person mask again.

"OK. So do whatever you like. I won't be waiting for you any longer."

"Kushala?" he said suddenly feeling very bad for her.

She looked up at him, no expression on her face. He didn't know what to say.

"Be strong, please. I am sorry," he said and escaped to 'his' apartment.

Once into the apartment, Anekand closed the door. Should he wait for Sati to return home? He so much wanted to meet her, see her. But his doppelganger would also return. And then what was he to say to them- who was he? Was he going to mention parallel universes? That concept, the physicist doppelganger could understand, but would these two understand? But then the doppelganger was Anekand- sorry of. So he might understand. But then again, the probability was less. He had no sister in any of the universes he had visited before. With such vast differences between those universes even when they were supposed to be parallel, Anekand doubted that his doppelganger and his sister would understand what parallel universes were. Moreover, the relationship between the brother and sister here was strung. So even if he met her, she wouldn't be happy seeing him. And then just out of the blue, he suddenly had a seemingly unrelated thought in which he realised that he was doing it all wrong. The wishing part before he travelled to parallel universes was all wrong. He had been stuck with the idea of choosing universes on the basis of profession- 'I wish to travel to a universe where I am a businessman', 'where I am a physicist', 'where I am a doctor'. Instead he should have been wishing to go to a universe where he had a sister, where she was alive or where she was dead; that should have been how he wished for. Next time, he would wish for something like that, he made a mental note of it, and sat down to meditate. But then he realised that wishing on those lines next time he travelled, might bring him back to this universe. And then how would he know if he was visiting an unvisited universe or this universe in which he was at the current moment. So he got up, found a pen and on the wall under the window, close to the floor, he wrote down 'Been here.' It was a tiny handwriting which no one would notice, but only he could because he knew where to look. He replaced the pen and sat to meditate. He returned home.

• • •

Next Day: Friday:

Anekand was excited to find a new wish statement and had been eager to use it. He was not visiting his office these last couple of days, but it was his own office; no one going to fire him from his own business. So he sat down to meditate at a time of the day when his doppelgangers would be off to work.

"I wish to go to a parallel universe, where I have a sister.'

He wanted to keep it simple.

Buzz.

Piercing silence.

Buzz.

Anekand opened his eyes and saw blue walls. The shade of blue was similar to the universe he had travelled to yesterday. He stood up and went to window. Then he bent down to look for the text he had written. It was there. 'Been here.' That meant this was the universe which was most similar to his home universe and which contained Sati. He re-meditated back home.

'I wish to go to the parallel universe where I have a sister, but I am not a businessman.'

Nothing happened- no buzz. That meant such a universe did not exist.

'I wish to go to the parallel universe where I have a sister, but she is dead.'

Again no buzz.

'I wish to go to a parallel universe where I have a sister, but which I have not yet visited.'

No buzz. The multiverse stubbornly refused to take him anywhere. What was happening?

'I wish to go to a universe where I have a sister and where her relationship with me is cordial.'

The multiverse didn't react this time too. Anekand snapped out of his meditation frustrated. Did all this imply that he had no sister in any other parallel universe except his home universe and the 'Been here' universe he had travelled to? That seemed to be the only plausible answer.

Anekand kept his frustration aside. He now mediated to converse with the universe. He told him about what he had wished, and how the multiverse had not taken him anywhere.

"Your deduction appears correct. There might be only two universes where your sister exists or existed."

"Then if I want to see her or meet her, I have no other option but to visit the universe where she and her brother are fighting a court case!"

"Yes."

"By the way, last time you told me about the buzz. The buzz in my ears is because the wormhole to another universe opens or remains open. But there is something else too that happens when I am travelling to another universe. There is a buzz at the start which I guess is because the wormhole opens. Then the buzz stops, and again it starts when I reach the other universe. The second buzz is because the wormhole remains open while I am still in a foreign universe. But between the first and the second buzz is a period of total silence. It's an ear-piercing silence. What is that?"

"That's the region between two universes. The silence that you experience is when you are out of one universe and not yet entered another universe. Even the buzz of the wormhole will stop. This is a region where nothing exists, where nothing can exist, where there are no physical laws, where there is neither time nor space, but where only pure consciousness can exist."

"But if nothing can exist in this region, how do I pass through from one universe to another?"

"You do not pass through this silent region, at least not the way you think you do. You leave your physical body at the end of the wormhole that reaches to the boundary of this universe; then your consciousness passes over to the corresponding wormhole of the universe you are going to. There, an exact copy of your physical body takes shape from the information contained in your consciousness."

"Does that mean I am dead and then I am resuscitated?"

"You are neither dead nor alive in the silent zone."

"This is incredible."

● ● ●

Next Few Days:

In the following days, Anekand didn't leap across universes. He wanted to see his sister, but at the same time, he didn't want to venture into the 'Been here' universe. And there was no other universe where Sati existed. He started imagining, or rather fantasising, scenarios in which he would go to that universe and find a solution to end the court fight. But where Kushala had failed to bring about reconciliation between them, he couldn't expect that his mediation would help. So this daydream was just that- a daydream. The other option was that may be he would go and meet his sister and tell her she need not despise him because he was her brother from another universe, that he missed her in his universe and would like to be in contact with her. But that would be a complicated thing to do, Anekand knew. It would be like going against himself as in against his doppelganger and supporting Sati, and from what Kushala had told him, it was not just his doppelganger's mistake that the relation between the brother-sister was strained. If only he could go to a time in that universe when they had not yet started fighting... And suddenly his thoughts stopped in their tracks. In fact, instead of going back in time in that universe, why not go back in time in his home universe? But was that possible? He would have to consult.

"Time-travel is not possible," said the universe.

"But there are scientific theories..."

"The debates may go on, but time-travel does not occur in any universe."

"Well, if it is scientifically impossible in one universe, then it won't happen in any universe because all the parallel universes have the same physical laws."

"Yes," said the universe, "time-travel is an impossibility wherever there are laws of physics."

"Then I will have to find a way to meet my sister in that one universe where she exists, and that too without letting my doppelganger in that universe know about it. Or I will have to find a way to mediate so that they can reconcile and I can meet both of them without any risk of landing myself into trouble."

"May be you will have to do that," the universe seemed to agree.

But it was easier said than done. Anekand couldn't really think of going to the 'Been here' universe except in his imaginations. It was already a complex situation and the relationship between the brother and the sister was so strained that Anekand's presence in that universe could only be seen by them as a threat as in competition to the inheritance.

Tuesday came along, and Anekand felt like visiting the universe where he was a librarian. Wednesday would surely be an off from work for the Kushala in that universe. That was the best encounter with any Kushala he ever had, and if he went to see her, he wouldn't even need to hide anything from her; she already knew he was from a different universe. The more he thought about visiting her, the more tempted he became to actually do it. But that would be betraying the librarian, Aseemand. In his mind, Anekand postponed, then cancelled, then again postponed his visit to that universe. He was just trying to convince himself to not to visit Kushala from that universe.

It was Wednesday now, and Anekand was all the more tempted to visit that Kushala from Aseemand's universe. But he went to office instead. He spent the day drowning himself into the routine. In the evening, he headed back home. He climbed the stairs to his apartment lost in his own world. But as he reached his floor, he was woken up from his thoughts by the noise of two people quarrelling. The sound came from Kushala's apartment. Suddenly, the door opened and a man came out.

"I have had enough of you," he said to Kushala as he walked by beside Anekand and went down the stairs.

Anekand looked at Kushala, but instantly looked away and kept walking through the corridor towards his apartment. Kushala closed the door. Anekand reached in his pocket and brought out his key.

"Anekand?" he heard a voice from behind.

He turned with the key still in his hand, and was surprised to find that the voice was Kushala's.

"Hi," he said.

"How have you been?" she asked.

"I am fine now. How are you?"

"You see how I am," Kushala said, her hand gesturing in the general direction of the stairs towards the man who had just left.

"I am sorry that I happened to return home at an awkward moment. He is...?"

"My husband," she said.

"Well, by-products of marriage," he said and smiled a bit trying to convey that her current situation, whatever it was, will pass.

She smiled back.

"But no," she said, "it's not just a by-product. I was never happy in this marriage."

Anekand became uncomfortable by this sudden candour from a person to whom he had not talked since his sister was murdered. He just stood there not knowing what to say or do.

"But," he finally said, "you got married recently. You both may require some time to adjust."

"No, no adjustment. If anything, it is a compromise. We have nothing in common. He doesn't have the brains to understand intellectual topics, nor the appreciation of art. He wants me to quit my job as an artist and join his business. I am an artist and my job is my passion. But you are a businessman too. Maybe you will feel he is right."

"No. Never," Anekand said emphatically. "If ever I get married, I wouldn't want my wife to quit her job if she likes it, to join my business. That decision would be hers and I would never expect quitting your job from an artist like you."

"So you understand?" she said.

"Yes, Kushala. I always understood," he said and then realised that he had alluded to their mutual attraction of the past.

"I got married in a hurry. I shouldn't have. But I didn't know whether I should have waited because I didn't know whether you did it," she said and her eyes widened as she realised what she had said and she covered her mouth in vain.

"What did I do?" asked Anekand.

"I didn't want to believe it, but I didn't know what to believe," she said, her hands still partially covering her mouth.

"What?" he asked already knowing what it was as he walked towards her.

"Did you kill her?" she asked directly.

"What do you think?"

"You tell me."

"Will you believe me?"

"I will."

"I didn't kill my sister," he said as he stopped right in front of her.

"Would you have told me if you had?"

"No, I wouldn't have, but I would have come to you and broken off whatever friendship we had because whatever I had felt for you had been in a sacred place in my heart, and I wouldn't have wanted you to be with a murderer. I would have known that I didn't deserve you, and I would have alienated myself from you."

Something suddenly nagged at him at the back of his mind. He didn't know what it was. 'Broken off.' 'Didn't deserve her.' Something kept nagging, but it was faint; it was a blur especially with her so close to him. Apart from her face, he couldn't see anything else. The subject of his sister's murder was brought up by someone who he had liked so much. He felt as if all his energy had drained.

"I am so sorry I didn't trust you at the time," Kushala said and touched his cheek.

"I understand; we weren't even the best of friends at that time."

"And now, at this moment, what are we?" her hand still caressing his cheek.

"I don't care to give, whatever we have right now, a name," he said and gently nudged her inside her apartment.

He held her face in his hands and kissed her. That was a real kiss for she was the real Kushala. She kissed him back as she reached for the door behind him and slammed it shut.

The next day, the excitement of the previous day was still there. Anekand woke up with a positivity which he had not felt since that fateful day a little more than a year back. For the first time since his depression, he had felt that he could let go of what had happened to him in the past, and look forward to the life in his future. He could now imagine his life with Kushala. A year had passed, but only a year. What she had done could be undone; it was not too late. She could undo her marriage, and he could marry her. Wait, he told himself; he was going too fast. Though through his encounters with Kushala in different universes he knew that in most universes, they would be happy with each other, Kushala of this universe couldn't be so sure about it. She had already committed a mistake of hurrying into a marriage and she would not tend to do it again. Moreover, he and Kushala weren't even now the best of friends even though the previous day had been special. And even if he was able to convince her that they were meant to be together, there would come a time when the pleasure-causing chemicals in the brain would slide down from their peak, and then the mystery and distress-causing thoughts of Sati's murder would come back to haunt him. But they would come back with or without Kushala in his life. So he knew he had to separate these two aspects of his life; his attraction to Kushala had to be separated from his memories of Sati. This was now getting complicated. Even thinking about it was getting complicated. He had to stop thinking about what happened with Kushala yesterday and concentrate on solving the mystery of his sister's murder. He would let Kushala decide what was best for them, and he would continue his search in different universes to find a clue to who might have murdered his sister. Even if Sati did not exist in any other universe except the 'Been here' universe, he may be able to get clues from those universes. May be, may be not. But he could try.

Just then the doorbell rang. Anekand opened the door.

"Kushala."

"Just wanted to ask... Do you regret what happened yesterday between us?"

"No. I have always liked you."

"Thank you. I had hoped that you would not regret it."

"That means you also don't have any qualms about it?"

"No, I don't."

"It's a relief to know that. Thanks."

Kushala left, and again Anekand felt a surge of hope about his future with her. But he didn't let that cloud his determination to find Sati's murderer. In fact, he realised that his encounter with Kushala had in a way made him stronger. The happy chemicals in his brain had lent him confidence which he had lacked since he had gone into depression. Should he tell Kushala about his meditation and his travel to other universes? And then he involuntarily imagined himself in conversation with Kushala telling her about how it had all begun with the consciousness of the universe contacting him. And then with him not realising that he was no longer having a mental conversation with Kushala, he unwittingly revisited his conversations with the universe and his experiences of the last few days. When he remembered his encounters with the Kushala's of the other universes, it occurred to him that telling the entire story of his travels to other universes to the real Kushala would be difficult. He then made a mental note that he would not indulge in telling her about all this until it became absolutely necessary, and he couldn't think of a scenario where he would require to tell her all of it.

Anekand, in his thoughts, reached the point where the universe had told him that time-travel was not possible.

'...time-travel does not occur in any universe.'

He could hear the voice of the universe saying that to him. He sighed. What he could do was essentially magic-travelling to other parallel universes, but ironically he couldn't do something that logically would seem much easier to do like travelling within his own universe to another time.

'...time-travel is an impossibility wherever there are laws of physics.'

And then, the laws of physics existed in all the universes, in every corner of every universe. And then it struck him like a bolt of lightning- the light of it illuminating the dark corners of his thoughts. Time-travel could not occur within any universe because of the laws of physics, but what about the silent region between universes which he required to pass through while travelling to other universes? It was a region where there were no laws of physics. Anekand's heart pounded in his chest as his brain devised the logic by which he could...

'I wish to go to the universe where my sister exists.'

Buzz.

And now the dead ear-piercing silence started taking over the buzz.

'I wish to go to the universe where my sister exists, and 940 days into the past.'

The silence ended and the buzz took over again. Anekand opened his eyes to the blue walls which were a different shade compared to his own apartment walls, but they looked plush now as if recently painted. He went towards the window and bent down to check whether the text 'Been here' existed. It didn't. Had he really time-travelled? He checked the wall-clock. There was no change in time. Then he checked the newspaper lying on the table. Anekand was ecstatic. He had indeed travelled around 2 years and 7 months into the past to the universe where Sati existed and to the time where the siblings were yet to get into a fight. Should he go to the doppelganger's office and see his sister? No. No. He hadn't thought of any plan. This was just a test drive. He had come here just to check whether he could travel through time. He sat to meditate again.

'I wish to go home.'

Buzz.

Silence.

'I wish to go to my home universe 940 days into the past.'

Anekand opened his eyes as the buzz subsided. He knew he had reached home, but wasn't sure about the time. He checked the newspaper, but was disappointed to find that he had reached his home time. That meant time-travel in his universe was not possible even through the silent zone.

He tried again- a slightly different way.

'I wish to go to the universe where my sister exists.'

Buzz.

Silence. Once in the silence zone, he tried to cheat.

'I wish to go to my home universe 940 days into the past.'

Buzz. And then the buzz subsided.

He opened his eyes to find that he was back in his own universe, but he had stubbornly stayed in his own time.

The Innervations connected all universes and through different times. This was because the universes were formed when decisions were taken. These decisions were the cause that split the universes into different parallel universes, and the effect was that the innervations ran through time as the individual universes progressed. The universes could be crossed over not only at the split but wherever the innervations reached and they reached throughout time. Hence, once Anekand was in the silent region, he could select which wormhole he intended to reach in the universe he was travelling to. This made the time-travel in the first test drive successful. When he reached the parallel universe, he had opened a wormhole. Till this wormhole closed, he could not travel to any other universe. So even when he tried to time-travel in the silent region during his return, the wormhole took him to his home time in the home universe. In the second test drive, he tried to cheat in the silent zone by dynamically changing the universe he wished for. He wished to go home but 940 days into the past. But this time too, he was brought back to his home time in the home universe. This was because once a wormhole was open in a universe for a person, no other wormhole could open for the same person in the same universe. Time-travel within the same universe indeed seemed impossible. But now Anekand at least could time-travel to another universe. As of now, he hadn't thought of an optimal plan to use it practically, but he would think. And for the first time in many days, he sat down to meditate not to talk to the universe or to leap to a parallel universe, but just to get his head clear.

Anekand's head was clear.

'I wish to go to the universe where I am a physicist.'

Grey walls. Anekand looked behind him at the sofa. The physicist wasn't there.

"Anyone home?"

Someone came out of the kitchen cautiously. It was the physicist.

"You again?" he said.

"Yes. Again."

Anekand told him everything. The events that he had imagined telling Kushala, he now instead narrated them to the physicist. And they also included the encounters with different Kushala's.

"If you ever come to this universe and even think of going to her apartment...."

"No, I don't plan to do that," said Anekand smiling. "I have already had an encounter with the Kushala in my universe."

"Oh. So you are on your leash now. Good."

Anekand continued his story and told his doppelganger about the time-travel.

"That was smart," said the physicist.

"I want you to do something for me. Have you ever leapt across universes?"

"What is your plan?"

"See," said Anekand, "the brick I told you about? It was lying on the road the day when my sister was murdered. If the brick hadn't been there, I would have taken the flyover. I had intended to. I took the road below instead because I didn't want anyone to get hurt in a freak accident. Had I taken the flyover, I would have reached home on time, and I would have been there with my sister. No one could have hurt her. I want you or someone to travel to that time and remove the brick from the road. As I told you, I can't do it myself as time-travel within my universe is not possible."

"The logic is fine, but the idea isn't," said the physicist. "What if the murderer finds you home and kills you as well? In your effort to save your sister, you end up dying yourself. The problem with your idea is that, you are not aware at that time when your sister was murdered that she would be. So you won't be alert. The murderer had entered your house without break-in. So he or she is a person you know. How was your sister killed?"

"Bullet."

"So how would the ignorant you of the past, who doesn't know that Sati was going to be killed with a bullet, save yourself and her from a seemingly friendly person wielding a gun?"

Anekand couldn't answer the question. His doppelganger was right.

"No one else's DNA was found in your house, right? And that's why they suspected you."

"Yes," said Anekand.

"The killer is too clever. And your presence, I think, will not undo your sister's murder. On the other hand, however, if I go there to you house, I might be able to save her as I know that a murder is going to take place."

"That would be risky. And I can't let you risk your life for the sister you never had."

"You will have to teach me how to make the leaps between universes."

"You don't know?"

"No. I was never into meditation."

"But then the first time I came here, you seemed not surprised at all. I thought that you might have done it yourself even if you are not a regular."

"The fact is, I was spooked when I saw you suddenly appear in my room. But I instantly realised that it was me from some other universe. I have a thesis in my name in which I theorise that it may be possible to leap to parallel universes through meditation."

"What? You figured it out just through logic?"

"And physics."

"And yet you never tried it yourself?"

"It's similar to your case. You know what enlightenment is, but as your universe told you, you are not enlightened."

"I guess you are right. But how did you know when I came here last time that I must be you from another universe?"

"If I have a thesis on travelling to parallel universes, a me from another universe could have figured it out, I thought, but I was disappointed to know that you are not a physicist."

"You and your physicist's arrogance..." Anekand said and smiled, and his doppelganger returned the smile.

"So this is a stalemate for me," Anekand added.

"Not necessarily. You can find someone from some universe who is good at those leaps, but again whoever goes there would be risking his life."

"If ever I solve this, I will return here and tell you."

"If ever you solve it, there are chances that you will not remember all this."

"What? What do you mean?"

"If you solve it, you would have most probably undone your sister's murder. Reality will change for you from that point onwards and that means all this never happens. For example, why would you look for your sister in different universes when she is alive in yours? Or why would you come to me? But that's a speculation that you may forget all of it. There is fifty percent probability of it. That's why I was telling you that the past version of you shouldn't take the risk of being home on the day of the murder because if the you in the past is killed, how can the current you exist? But as I said, these are speculations, and there are chances that you will still remember it as a parallel reality. Again, that too, a speculation."

Anekand returned to his own universe. He now had more to think after talking to his physicist doppelganger. The scientist was right. Logically, if he ever solved the mystery and undid Sati's murder, he may not remember a thing. The level he had achieved in his meditation was wonderful. He could talk to the universe now. All this he might forget. Along with the other Kushala's, he might also forget the encounter with the real Kushala. But his sister would be alive. Whatever he would lose, he might achieve it again. His meditation might make him talk to the universe again. Moreover, if his sister never got murdered, it would also mean that Kushala might never get alienated from him and consequently not get married to her present husband. Anekand had to solve it. The lives of three persons, including himself, depended on it.

CHAPTER II

The Answers:

All answers lie within your own self. That was a statement always associated with the yogic meditation. You can know the remotest of things if you concentrate on a problem hard enough. The thing is, that was not only true for meditation, but also true about logic. The deeper anyone thinks on a logical question, the probability to find the answer, increases. Anekand knew meditation, and he also had a logical brain. In the days that followed after his revisit to the physicist's universe, he thought about the problem not only through meditation, but from a different perspective- logic.

Basically, Anekand kept repeatedly thinking about the event of the murder, the proofs, the motive, the evidence and the lack of it, and after that one year of depression his conversations with the universe, his own leaps across universes, the time-travel and finally his little chat with the physicist. He thought it all without putting any pressure on himself to find the answers. He wanted the answers, but the direct method of delving into the problem had until now proved unsuccessful. So by repeatedly thinking about the events without really trying to find anything in them, he was allowing the answers to come to him passively through the subconscious.

In a couple of days, Anekand had gathered bits of information, which he had already known earlier too but hadn't connected them to one another. He now placed them in new places in his mind and sew them into a collage. The collage formed a vivid picture. The image this collage formed in his mind might be the fact or not, but at least now he had a theory to who might have killed Sati. Now he was going to travel to a parallel universe. If the multiverse took him to the universe he thought it would take him, then he could test his theory further. If the multiverse took him to another universe, then he might have to tweak his theory. And thus, he sat down to meditate.

'I wish to go to a universe where the Anekand in that universe can leap to other universes.'

Buzz.

Silence.

Buzz.

Anekand opened his eyes, stood up, searched the apartment for the thing he was looking for. He found it. He then returned home quietly.

Strike one.

Speculation seemed correct.

He then closed his eyes and wished to leap to a universe again in which the Anekand of the universe could make the leaps, but he also wished that this universe could not be the one he was taken to in the previous attempt. This time nothing happened- he stayed in his home universe. So he concluded that there was only one universe apart from his own where Anekand could make the leaps. Then he made his third wish with a different condition. This time the multiverse took him to the universe he had travelled to just a few minutes back. He now knew that his collage stood all the three tests. Yet his theory may in time prove to be wrong, but at the moment, everything seemed to go as he had guessed it would. And now was the difficult part. Execution.

• • •

Execution:

Sati was gagged and tied to a chair in her bedroom. The bedroom door was closed. Once in a while, the sound of her struggle to get free could be heard outside the room in the hall. But it was in vain. She, in her bouts of desperation, did nothing more than shift her chair a bit here and there. In the hall, Sati's brother was at gunpoint, and behind the gun was Anekand. He had procured the pistol from the black market in his home universe. He was a businessman, and though he had always kept himself away from the dark facets of being in business, he was still able to get himself a gun almost as soon as he had wanted it.

"So?" said Anekand to his doppelganger.

Anekand had entered this universe at a time in the evening when both the brother-sister duo would be at office. Then he had remained hidden in Sati's bedroom. When she entered the room, he had simply held her at gunpoint and gagged her and then tied her to a chair. Then he had gone out into the hall, and had pointed the pistol at his businessman doppelganger of this universe. Both were now seated at the opposite ends of the sofa.

"What do you want?" asked the doppelganger.

"I want some answers."

"Why have you held my sister hostage?"

"Don't ask dumb questions. I don't want anything from her, but she is not free to go unless I have the answers. And moreover, what do you care? You two are in legal battle. Oh! Got it! If I kill her, then the police will suspect you, won't they? You can escape to another universe, but then your property and money will remain here."

The doppelganger didn't say anything.

"So, you can leap to other universes!" said Anekand. "Don't try to escape now. I can come behind you at the same speed. You may wonder how I would know which universe you escape to. But that won't matter if I wish for the universe you went to. I will be just behind you. And be informed, I have become a kind of expert in those things for some days now."

"What do you want?"

"The truth. Did you kill my sister by coming to my universe?" Anekand came directly to the point.

The doppelganger hesitated looking alternately at the gun and at Anekand.

"Don't worry," said Anekand. "I won't kill you as long as you give me answers."

"I..." the doppelganger still hesitated.

"You will make this hard for yourself if you don't answer. Trust me, I will tell your sister what you did and Kushala too."

"No," said the doppelganger.

"OK then. Speak."

"I killed your sister."

Anekand's grip on the weapon tightened. Seeing this, his doppelganger lifted his hands in surrender and thus pleaded to the man with the gun to not to shoot.

"Why?" demanded Anekand.

"It was anger."

"At my sister?"

"No, at mine."

"I have been thinking about it, and I have not been able to answer those questions myself. I had guessed you did it, but the motive isn't clear," said Anekand.

"As you know we are in a legal battle. It started two years ago. One year later, when my anger reached its peak, I procured a gun from the black market, chose a universe where Sati existed, and shot her the moment I saw her.

Then I tried and tried to return to my universe here, but I kept failing. I couldn't meditate, not after I had killed a human being. But in the end, I managed and escaped. I regretted killing her the moment I did it, but till then I had lost total control over myself. The dispute between me and my sister had started when my client called KA Logistics preferred Sati's services over mine."

"Wait," said Anekand. "KA Logistics, you said?"

On the day Sati died, Anekand was with a client- KA Logistics- to make a deal. Thoughts stormed in his mind. What if after closing the deal, this client would have specifically asked for Sati's services and not his. Would that have led to the same events that happened in this universe? No, no, he thought. He loved his sister. He wouldn't have imagined that she would go behind his back to woo his client. So even if the client had preferred Sati over Anekand, he would have let it happen cordially. In this universe, the conditions must have been different. There could have been a lack of trust between the brother-sister even before KA Logistics.

"Yes, KA Logistics," replied the doppelganger. "He is in your universe too?"

"That doesn't matter. Continue."

"A year later the distrust had reached its peak. I was into meditation for a long time since my childhood and one year before the fight between Sati and me started, I had already made a leap to another universe."

Anekand remembered his universe telling him that he was the first one to converse with the consciousness of the universe. So that meant this doppelganger had made the leap without conversing with his universe. He must have been good; he had discovered the leaps without the universe suggesting him about them.

"But why come to my universe and kill my sister?"Anekand asked.

"I don't know why your universe was selected. May be the multiverse selects universes that we travel to at random, and sometimes it lets us go back to the same universe. But you would already know that."

"So you really don't know or are you lying?"

"Lying? About what?" asked the doppelganger.

Anekand looked into his opponent's eyes. He genuinely seemed not to know.

"You never really got to the why's and how's of the parallel universes, did you?" said Anekand.

"I don't know what you mean?"

"When you came to my universe and murdered Sati, you didn't know why my universe was selected by the multiverse," said Anekand and wondered whether the doppelganger still had no contact with the consciousness of the universe.

"No. I just wished for a universe in which Sati existed because all universes don't contain Sati."

"So you knew all universes didn't contain Sati, but you didn't know that ours are the only two universes that contain Sati."

"No, I didn't," said the doppelganger, and he seemed lost in thought.

"But that wouldn't have mattered. You would have still come and murdered her."

"No. In fact, if I had known that, I might not have."

Anekand looked at him questioningly.

"You asked me why I went to your universe and killed Sati. Hear me out. I wanted to kill my own sister, but for obvious reasons, I couldn't. The police would find motive and in course of time, they would dig out any false alibi that

I would present. So killing my own sister in my universe would implicate me and they would convict me eventually. Now consider this fact- parallel universes though different, run parallel to one another in many ways. If I killed a Sati in a parallel universe, it would increase the probability of some Anekand from some universe coming to my universe and killing the Sati in this universe. I thought I was doing some other Anekand a favour that I myself wanted in this universe. Someone else would kill my sister, Sati, the way I killed some Sati in some universe. I could have a real alibi and a real killer which the police would never find, and thus I would eventually be acquitted leaving all the property to myself. What happened to you? You too were acquitted, right?"

Anekand, at that moment, felt utter hatred for his doppelganger. But at the same time, he realised that he was intelligent and logical. He had devised a perfect murder, in which he would never get caught and the Anekand in that other universe, where Sati would be murdered, would also get acquitted. This would leave the entire property to him. Anekand's doppelganger was right in thinking that if he killed a Sati from a parallel universe, some Anekand from some other universe would come and kill his Sati from this universe. But unfortunately for Anekand's doppelganger, he didn't know that only two universes existed which contained Sati.

"Yes, I got acquitted," Anekand replied.

"In fact, when I saw you here with the gun, I thought that my plan was working, that you had come to kill Sati. But I don't want that. I don't want her to die. I regret killing your sister. I was wrong. I have never forgiven myself for that."

"And yet you continue your legal battle with your sister?"

"I don't want that too. I am doing it because I took someone's life and if I had conceded my share of the property here in this universe, it would mean the Sati who I killed died in vain, for nothing. I didn't know what to do. So I continued."

"And you broke up with Kushala."

"Yes. I don't deserve her. Wait. How do you know that?"

"I was here before."

"But how did you know I killed your sister?"

"Firstly, the police didn't find any evidence of forced entry. So it was someone who my sister knew. I was thinking on those lines when I realised that if my doppelganger from another universe travelled to my universe, he wouldn't have to knock on the door. He would be inside the apartment when he made the leap. Secondly, the police didn't find any other DNA that could point to a murderer. My doppelganger from any parallel universe would probably have my own DNA. These two facts made me think that Sati's murderer was me from some other universe. Having thought of that, I made a wish to enter a universe where my doppelganger could leap across universes. I was sent here by the multiverse. I have written here on the wall there 'Been here.' So when I was sent here, I knew that the multiverse had sent me to a universe where this universe's Anekand is in a legal battle with his sister. I then tried again to enter a universe which was not your universe but where my doppelganger could leap, but nothing happened. That meant that we are the only two versions of ourselves who can make the leap. I also wished for a third time. This time I wished to go to a parallel universe where my doppelganger had or has a gun. I was brought here again. That was when I became almost sure that you were the one who killed my sister. But I didn't know why. Now, I know."

"If I had known," said the doppelganger, "that we were the only ones who could make the leaps, I might not have killed your sister because having only two universes in the multiverse with universe-leaping Anekand's would decrease the probability of my sister's murder to almost nil. And yes, I also hadn't thought of our DNAs being a perfect match. Had I known it, that would have been a deterrent in my plan because finding the DNA of a third person at the site of murder was an essential part of my plan. I am extremely sorry that I killed your sister. I am sorry that I killed any person at all. If only I could undo it! And yes, though I fear for my life, you can kill me and end my life of shame and regret. Please do it. It becomes unbearable most of the times. Please end this. You will only do me a favour. My sister cannot be suspected of my murder as she is gagged and tied, is it not?"

Tears started rolling down the doppelganger's cheeks. And in spite of everything, Anekand felt a tiny bit of sympathy for him.

Anekand looked at his doppelganger. He had closed his eyes anticipating that he would be killed any moment now. Anekand purposely made a sound of the safety of the gun; he wanted to see the reaction of that sound on the man in front of him. All the muscles in his body became taut and creases developed on his eyelids as he closed his eyes more tightly as if they were going to close his ears too and protect him from the approaching sound of his own death. Anekand was enjoying it, and then he chuckled. Hearing that sound, the doppelganger frowned but still didn't open his eyes. But after a moment or two, his curiosity gave him the courage and slowly he opened his eyes. Anekand had put the gun away. The doppelganger looked at him confused.

"Why? Why haven't you killed me?"

"You said if possible, you could have undone it."

"No one can bring the dead back to life."

"Oh! Then you must have meant resurrection when you said undoing the event, but I took it literally. But how could you mean resuscitation when in our culture, we cremate the dead and when there is no physical body to resurrect?"

"Why are you going into technicalities, and why did you laugh?"

"I laughed looking at you- all your creased face. You looked constipated. You know I can't forgive you for what you did. When you killed my sister, she must have seen your face. And in her death, she must have thought I killed her. But the question of forgiveness doesn't arise if the murder never occurred."

"No, no. Wait. I couldn't have done that with my face exposed. My face was covered. I couldn't risk anyone seeing me and thinking that you did it because that would mean if anyone from a parallel universe came to kill my sister, he would also have his face exposed most probably, and that would end up proving that I killed my sister. Moreover, if you had been there with her at the time I came, you would have come to know that I am you from another universe; I mean there was a possibility that you would know. I didn't want that to happen too."

"You really did plan it, didn't you?"

"I am not proud about it, but yes, I had thought over it logically. But wait. What do you mean all that thing about resurrect and undo? And what about no question of forgiveness?"

"If given a chance, will you undo what you did?"

"Yes..." the doppelganger said tentatively; he didn't know what Anekand was thinking.

"You can undo it. In principle, it is possible."

The doppelganger looked at Anekand incredulously.

"What do you mean?" he asked.

Anekand explained that time-travel within a universe was not possible. But you could go to another time in another universe. He then explained how he had done it through the silent region.

"OK. That is new to me. I never knew it and I never thought of it. But what do you want me to do?"

"I give you two options," said Anekand. "The first one is that you go to the same day when you murdered my sister and stop yourself of the past from committing the murder. What do you say?"

"I would like to hear the second option as well."

"The second option is that you go to the same day of the murder, but a few minutes early. At that time there would be no one in my apartment. Then you go to the flyover of the highway, the one which we take when are travelling back from office. You will require to go to the office-end of the flyover. On the road below the flyover, you will see a brick. You just have to pick it up and throw it away to the side of the road."

"What? How will that help?"

Anekand explained how he had seen the brick and to prevent an accident, he had turned his car away from the flyover. Then since he had taken the road below, he had thought of visiting the client's office which was on the way.

"KA Logistics?" enquired the doppelganger.

"Yes."

"It's an irony that the client which led to my thoughts of murder in my universe was responsible to complete that very thought in your universe. So you reckon that if you hadn't taken the flyover, you would have got home early and you would have protected your sister?"

"Yes. But that means I also put my life in danger for your might kill me too."

"No. Can't you see it? I can't kill you. You should know my train of thoughts by now. I can't kill you because the younger me would think that if you are killed while your sister is killed, a different doppelganger would kill me when he kills my sister."

"So you think my sister won't be murdered by your past-self if I am there?"

"No. I had thought that even if you are there, I would kill your sister."

"In that case, you will have to take the first option; you will have to go and stop yourself from killing my sister."

"But that would mean I can die," said the doppelganger.

"You can take your gun."

"And if I from the future, that is the current me, kills myself from the past, I don't exist and if I don't exist, how will I stop my past-self from killing your sister? That's an endless loop. A paradox. I can't kill my past-self. And if he kills me while saving your sister, the crime will still be committed. I die and your sister dies too. I can try and dissuade him from doing it. I would tell him that he doesn't really want to do it, but my past-self is so much filled with rage at the moment or even in those days before he commits the murder that there is a high probability that I will fail. That is because he will be in no mood to listen to anyone. I can carry a gun but without bullets and hold him at gunpoint and then try to dissuade him."

"Will that work?"

"I don't know. I should have my face covered too because if he knows I am his future-self, I risk letting him know too much about his future, but the main risk is of collapsing of the multiverse because of the paradox of the future self meeting his past self."

"You talk like a physicist," said Anekand.

"You know more about leaping across universes, but that does not make me less intelligent than you. You had motivation to learn more about leaps because your sister was killed. It's just that. So where was I? Yes. I should have my face covered, but the problem with that is he won't know who I am, and he may risk shooting me even if he is at gunpoint."

"But you may not have your face covered and pose as me."

"But that too, even if he doesn't know that I am not you, will lead to self meeting self paradox because I will be meeting my own past self. When I am stopping my past-self from killing your sister, I will have no memory of anyone stopping me from doing it when I actually committed the crime. This may lead to me having contradictory memories about the event. This will happen because of the dynamic change of reality in your universe or in the multiverse, and the plan may just flop because I in my current version will become too confused and disoriented to carry out the plan successfully. It's is too unpredictable. And all this- only if the multiverse doesn't collapse because of the paradox. So no, I can't go and stop my past-self. You have a third option?"

Anekand thought for a while considering all that they had discussed.

"There is one," he said finally. "But that too may not result in what we intend," said Anekand. "Your past-self may still commit the crime."

"Tell me," demanded Anekand's doppelganger.

"Let me enlist a few facts. There are only two of us who can make the leaps. I cannot time-travel in my own universe and stop you from killing my sister. You can go back in time in my universe, but you cannot directly stop your past-self from killing my sister because that will lead to paradoxes, and as the reality changes dynamically, you will have conflicting memories and you may start feeling confused and disoriented to the point that you may not be able to stop the crime from happening. So that leaves only one option. My past-self. My past-self is in the least danger of being killed by your past-self as you have made it clear. You have also made it clear that once you killed my sister, at that moment you regretted doing it. There was always some part of you who loved your own sister. I want to make use of that."

"Tell me the plan," said the doppelganger again.

Anekand explained the plan.

"Now go and untie your sister. She hasn't seen my face. I had my face covered too," said Anekand.

The doppelganger nodded.

"Good luck with the execution of the plan," Anekand said. "This is your only chance to undo what you did and my only chance to have my sister back."

He then sat down to meditate, and left for his home universe. The doppelganger opened the room to find his sister gagged and tied to a chair. She had long quit struggling to free herself. He went towards her and gently un-gagged her. She coughed as fresh air reached her lungs.

"Who was he? Did you hire him to kill me?" she demanded still tied to the chair.

"No."

"Then what did he want?"

"He was a ghost from my past. All's well now. I hope so."

He freed her arms and legs. Sati stretched her hands and legs.

"Tell me who he was. Should I call the police?" she asked.

"If I had wanted the police, I would have called them myself."

He sat down on the floor in front of her chair and placed his hands on her knees. She was perplexed by this gesture.

"I am sorry for everything," he said. "I don't care whether you went behind my back to KA Logistics. I don't care about the money. I don't care about the court case. I will back off immediately from the case. I don't care about my ego. You are my sister and I love you. It's liberating to say that and feel that after a long time, but that feeling had always been there hidden somewhere beyond reach of all the superficial things for which I was fighting against you. If you want the entire business, take it. I am done."

"I never wanted the entire business. I admit I went to KA Logistics, but that was because I had lost my confidence. You brought in most of the clients and that had left me feeling insecure about my own abilities. What I did was a mistake. If I had known that thing would escalate to this point, I would have never done it."

He got up and pulled her up from the chair and hugged her. She hugged him too and smiled with teary eyes.

• • •

• • •

The Day of Murder:

The businessman Anekand from the 'Been here' universe had leapt over to Anekand's universe, not in the present but to the day the murder was committed. He had reached a time of that was much earlier than when his past-self had reached. The apartment was empty. He opened the door and went out, his hat blocking his face from most eyes.

He reached his destination- the point where the flyover started. He looked around and found the brick. He knew that that was the redundant part of the plan, but he still picked it up and threw it by the side of the road. Though redundant in the plan itself, it was a good thing to do. He then went to a mobile phone store and got a cheap phone and an instant connection; his original phone from the future and from a different universe showed network but did not connect. This man from the future then called up Anekand of the past from his cheap phone.

"I want to meet you, sir. I represent your client, KA Logistics. I want to discuss business. I will meet you at your apartment in half an hour."

"Please come to my office. I was going to deliver a letter to your managers."

"No, I can't come to your office. This meeting is unofficial; my boss wants to discuss business unofficially before proceeding officially."

"But..."

"It's important. I want to share some information. Will just take ten minutes of your time. Please it's important. And please meet me in half an hour because my boss wants to visit you in your office tomorrow if today's meeting is successful. I just work for my boss and he asked me to visit you and not discuss anything on phone. That's why I want to meet you personally. It's my personal request that I am asking you to meet you in half an hour because I have some personal commitments today which I won't be able to attend to if I am delayed by our meeting. Please, it's a request."

Anekand sighed. With all that 'please' and 'request you' thing of this poor employee of some tyrant boss, Anekand agreed. The doppelganger was relieved- Anekand of the future had been correct in telling him that if he sounded all needy, he will convince the younger Anekand to meet him. The plan was basically to ensure that Anekand reached home in time.

The doppelganger waited outside the building. Once he saw Anekand's car from a distance, he went in, covered his face with a handkerchief; the large hat was already there to conceal most of his head. He then waited on the flight of stairs that led to the floor above Anekand's apartment. Anekand came and approached his apartment. As soon as the door opened, the doppelganger strode towards Anekand and pushed him inside. He brought out his gun, which only he knew was empty, and pointed it at Anekand.

"Hey! What do you want?" asked Anekand raising his hands up.

"I want nothing from you," said the doppelganger.

Sati was there in the hall. She froze too.

"Trust me, I am here to help. Please do exactly as I say and she will live."

"What do you mean?"

"I am there one who spoke to you just now on the phone," said the doppelganger. "A man is coming here to murder Sati. I won't be able to stop that man. Only you can, Anekand. Now, both of you go into the bedroom."

They complied with the gun still pointed at them.

"If you are here to help, why are you pointing that gun at us?" asked Sati.

Once in the room, the man from the future handed over the gun to Anekand.

"See for yourself. The gun is empty."

Anekand was confused.

"Now trust me, I am here to help," he closed the door to the bedroom. "A man will be here in about five minutes. Once he is here, you, Anekand, will have to go out. Not a minute before that."

"We can take him by surprise or at least can call the police," argued Anekand.

"That's what I don't want. If you attack him or call the police, trust me he will come back for Sati when he is free. If you don't listen to me, you two will have to live your future lives continuously watching your back."

"What has she done to him?"

"Nothing. He is a psychopath. Mentally unstable."

"What is your plan?"

"You just have to tell him that you love your sister but not before he shows his intention to kill her. He will not kill you. Be assured of that."

"I tell him that and he will go?"

"If he doesn't, tell him he will regret killing Sati all his life. He won't be able to forgive himself. And that if he kills Sati, you as her brother won't be able face your own self or Kushala all your life."

"What? Where did Kushala come here from? And how do you know us or Kushala?"

"No time to explain. Less than five minutes. You just need to know that he's a psychopath. You will have to deal with him psychologically."

"And you are sure he won't kill me?"

"Yes, he sees to it that a man is not hurt when a sister is dead."

"Did his sister betray him?" asked Sati.

"Yes. Long story. But trust me, this is his first time and he won't try to kill anyone else in future if you convince him that your brother-sister love is real."

"This all sounds fantastic," commented Sati.

"And why can't you help when he's here?"

"If he suspects the involvement of a third person, he may go berserk."

"You are just assuming all will go well with this madman if he is convinced that our brother-sister love is real."

"I know for sure," said the doppelganger. "I have to leave now. Remember; don't go out till the time I told you."

"Why is time that important?"

"He believes in astrology and if you try to stop him at a certain time, he will believe that his mission is jinxed, and that will help you."

"Show me your face."

"No. I fear for my life."

"All this sounds ridiculous."

"Then don't believe me and risk Sati's life."

"How will he enter the apartment?"

"He has his methods. I am taking my gun back. You can solve this problem only through non-violence. He shouldn't sense that he is threatened," saying that, the doppelganger took back his gun, left the room and the apartment, went to the stairs and meditated.

He couldn't believe all the lies he had come up with. Some of them had been suggested by Anekand of the future, but many of them, he himself had come up with at the spur of the moment. He didn't know he was capable of making things up to such an extent- astrology, jinx and what not. The lies were a part of his and the future Anekand's plan. The younger Anekand should not know more than that was actually essential to save Sati. That was because the younger man still hadn't had his experience with the consciousness of the universe and the leaps across universes. He required to discover all that by himself. That was the reason he was told not to go back to the hall till a certain time because if he did, he would see a man conjuring up in his apartment. Apart from the shock he would receive and then mess up the task of saving Sati, he would also come to know (later- when he would think about it) about the consciousness of the universe and parallel universes because of something he was not supposed to see. The police could not be involved too. The reality about parallel universes could not be shared with the general public. Moreover, after his escape from the police which would just be a disappearing act for him through meditation, the murderer would definitely return to this universe to complete his task. There was only one way he could be stopped, and that was to invoke his love for his sister. As of now, the man from the future concentrated on his meditation.

Buzz. He was back to the future.

Back at the apartment, Anekand and Sati stayed hidden inside the bedroom. They were in two minds whether to go out and take the coming intruder by surprise or to follow what was told to them. But they didn't have much time to think. They suspected that they were told about the intruder so late on purpose so that they would have the least time to think, and then most probably they would follow what they had been told to. And now, the time had come. Anekand heard something in the hall and his heart started pounding in his chest. With a slight tremble in his hands, he opened the door and stepped out. The man in front of him had his face covered, and for a moment, Anekand thought it was the same man who had come to help them, but then he realised that the clothes were different. Anekand raised his hands as the trespasser pointed his gun at him. Anekand noticed the gun too was quite similar to the one he had just seen. May be the same make, but that wasn't important at the moment.

"What do you want?" asked Anekand.

"Nothing from you. You stay away and I won't hurt you."

"You want money?"

"Shut up. Where is your sister?"

"What do you want from her?"

"Is she in that room?" the masked man came forward.

Anekand came between him and the bedroom.

"Move aside," said the trespasser.

"I can't. She's my sister."

"You see this gun, right? How do you think you can save her from me?"

"I may die trying to stop you, but that's what I will do."

The doppelganger hesitated a bit as he saw this version of himself from this universe who was willing to risk his life for his sister, and there he himself was trying to kill a sister so that someone else would do it for him back in his own universe. Suddenly, he felt ashamed of himself and that made him angry.

"Move or I will kill you too."

Hearing that, Sati stormed out of the room.

"No," she screamed. "Don't hurt him, please."

"Sati! What are you doing? Go back in."

Sati didn't go back in. She came and stood beside her brother.

"Why?" said Anekand to Sati. "Why did you come out?"

"You want to kill me, right?" Sati said the masked man. "So, I am here now. You don't have to hurt him. We have not seen your face. So, he won't be able to tell anything to the police. You don't have to hurt him."

She started sobbing. The trespasser seemed confused. This sister risked her life by coming out of the room so that her brother could stay alive. She loved him. Sati loved Anekand. Anekand loved his sister. Suddenly, the doppelganger was overcome by emotion. What was he doing? This rage! Why this rage? His anger had grown continuously in the past few days and for the last couple of days, it had surpassed the level that he could bear. In that state of mind, he had devised a way to get rid of his sister by killing a sister from another universe. What was he doing? He couldn't believe he was doing it. He had come here to kill an actual person! A person who was alive now- a person who would be dead because of him. A person who had done nothing wrong to him or even to her brother. He was wrong. The sister in this universe wasn't going to betray her brother. And in his own universe... had Sati betrayed him really or was it just a big misunderstanding. Looking at this Sati in front of him, he was no longer sure that the version of this person in his universe had intentionally betrayed him. He lowered his gun and sat down with his head buried in his hands. Anekand and Sati looked at each other, not believing that the stranger's idea was really working on this mentally unstable person. Was this man convinced enough so as not to carry out the murder he had planned to commit? The man in front of them rose up.

"I am sorry. I need to go home to my sister."

He then left the apartment and went to the stairs where he sat down in a yogic pose and disappeared to his own universe. Anekand and Sati had a few questions, but no one dared to ask them to the mad man.

• • •

The Present:

Anekand was sitting on his sofa in the hall after a day of work, and suddenly he went faint. His vision blurred and he almost fell to the floor. He held his forehead as his head throbbed. And then nothing. All this stopped as suddenly as it had started. But it felt odd. Really odd. He didn't know for sure whether this was real or he was in a dream.

"Anekand?" he heard a voice and looked in the direction of its source. "Are you OK?"

Sati came and touched him on the shoulder.

"Sati? Sati!"

"Is something wrong?"

"No. Nothing. Suddenly felt drained of all energy."

"Don't work too hard. You should get some rest too," she said and started walking towards her room.

"Don't go. Sit. Talk."

Sati smiled and sat down on one of the chairs adjacent to the sofa.

"Say."

They talked as they usually did. When Anekand asked his sister to sit and talk, one part of his mind felt as if he had not talked to her for a long time, but the other part felt as if he hadn't missed anything. It was an odd feeling. But whatever game his mind was playing on him, he felt good talking to his sister. But still, there was some confusion. It felt chaotic. He could talk to Sati normally, but he was surprised that he could. It was as if he wasn't supposed to know things that he knew, and yet those were his own memories. Odd. Soon, he retired for the day.

The dreams at night were bizarre. They made no head or tail, and Anekand couldn't remember anything in the morning except that he had dreamt much more than usual. As sleep ebbed and wakefulness took its place, the confusion started. Sati was dead. No, what was he thinking? How could he think such a thing about his sister? She was good and well, and he could hear her presence at this moment somewhere in the apartment. Then why was he feeling the pain of her death as well extreme joy that she was alive? What kind of....? And then the dust of his memories settled as he cleared his mind. The dust had come from two sets of memories. As he consciously segregated the dust and assigned them to their respective sets, he remembered and realised what kind of feat he and his doppelganger of the 'Been here' universe had achieved.

Anekand was still in bed in his room. He was eager to talk to the universe. So he sat up and started meditating.

"You have changed me," said the universe.

"Yes," said Anekand. "I have changed myself too. I would like to hear the 'how' from you."

"My memories cannot explain what you did, not quite neatly anyway. But your memories might," said the universe.

And so Anekand tried to explain.

A choice usually split a single universe into two parallel universes, but with the choice Anekand had taken and with the ensuing time-travel, two separated parallel universes had merged into one. The two versions of the same person from two different universes had managed to change the reality and even rearrange the point of the split. The initial split had taken place where Anekand had picked up the brick and then had gone to meet his client at KA Logistics. Now the split was shifted a bit earlier in time. In one of the universes, he had received a call from a stranger (the time-travelling doppelganger from the 'Been here' universe), and in the other Anekand had received no such call. In the absence of that call, he had gone home to find his sister dead. In the other universe, a 'psychopath' was convinced not to kill Sati, but because Anekand of the currently merged universe had both the sets of memories, he knew who the caller was and also who the psychopath was- it was the same person but from two different times. The split universes continued their separate courses for around a year. At the end of that year, Anekand from the split universe where Sati was dead, met his doppelganger from another parallel universe (the 'Been here' universe), and events thereafter involving time-travel, had made the recently spilt universes to merge.

The same fate of merger applied to the 'Been here' universe as well. In one of the 'Been here' universes, the doppelganger killed Sati, and in the other, he was convinced not to. In the present, now, the universes merged, and the doppelganger too felt confused for some time after which he realised what had happened. He had undone his crime with help of Anekand whose sister he had murdered. The court case was withdrawn and the brother-sister duo was happy that the feud was over. The doppelganger had resumed his relationship with Kushala of that universe.

Anekand from the home universe, in the present time, opened his eyes after this explanation to the universe. Kushala was on his mind now. He remembered that his plan to meet her at her artists' gallery had manifested a year ago. That had been the beginning of their real friendship. His visits to her gallery had increased in frequency, and they used to talk on their way home. The man who she had married in the split universe never came in her life in the current reality, and at the current moment, Kushala as well as Anekand knew that they felt more than friendship for each other, but both hadn't had the nerve to say it. Their relationship for the past one year had been romantic only in their minds. But now, it was time, Anekand decided. In fact, it was high time. He quickly took a bath, cleaned up, freshened up, told Sati that he might skip office today and left the apartment. He didn't have to go far. He just had to ring the bell to Kushala's apartment. He hesitated, but only for a moment. Kushala opened the door.

"Anekand! You know I had the weirdest of dreams. I felt as if I was married to this man- some weird man who wanted me to quit my job... oh... and in that dream something happened to Sati. It was a nightmare. It was odd. Now that I am awake, I know it was just a dream but it still feels so real."

"I know."

"You know?"

"I mean we all have such odd and vivid dreams once in a while," Anekand said.

He knew that, for all people who had known that Sati had been murdered, today would be a weird day as they would struggle to find what exactly the fact was. But since Sati was now alive, they would all brush off their other set of memories as a dream. Some would not even remember these memories. Some would be confused as we all are sometimes when we think a person is dead, but in fact he or she isn't, and then we shrug and think it must have been our imagination or our brains must have related someone else's death to this person who in fact is alive. We never think more than once about our confusion. We just accept the current fact that the concerned person is alive and move on. Anekand knew this would happen to some of the people involved, but there would be no discussion over it. How would you talk about something like this to anyone? Would it be like 'That girl living in 4402 was dead, right? Till yesterday? And now she's alive. At least I thought she was dead, but now I am not so sure. How come?' Most people cannot remember the other set of memories when the current facts are in front of them, and they would laugh at the person who says such things. Anekand knew, no one would ever suspect about parallel universes. Anyway, no one would remember all the details of the bygone year for their own lives would have remained unchanged. As for Sati, she was the only person involved who would have no so-called nightmares or confusion for she would have only one set of memories because in one of the spilt universes, she didn't exist.

"What are you thinking?" said Kushala bringing Anekand back in the moment. "I am sorry. You must have come here for something, and I just started talking to you about my nightmare."

"No," said Anekand, "it's OK. You were two, now you are one."

Kushala frowned. She didn't know what she had just heard. She just stared at him. Anekand realised he had said something that sounded odd.

"In your dreams, you are a different person. When you get up you try to find out what's real and what's not. Just that," he tried to cover up.

"OK," she smiled. "Well, what brought you here at the start of the day?"

Anekand realised that he had lost his nerve again. He couldn't think of anything to say. He just stood there breathing deeply to calm himself down and in the process just stared at Kushala. She became self-conscious.

"What? Say," she said, but it was just a whisper as she sort of anticipated the reason why Anekand was standing in front of her.

"Nothing. I will come back later," he turned, but she grabbed him by his hand and tugged at it suggesting that he come in.

He did. She closed the door shut. Anekand swallowed air as she raised her hand and touched his cheek. But then his lips parted. He let go of every thought and held her face in his hands. She wrapped her arms around him, and they kissed for the first time in this reality. No words would have said what their unsaying lips said to each other. Some memories from some other universes flashed in Anekand's mind as they continued to kiss, but they vanished as Kushala tore away from him and then pulled him with her into her bedroom as he realised today was Wednesday.

• • •

Epilogue:

Anekand visited the 'Been here' universe to thank his doppelganger.

"I must be the one who should be thanking you. You helped me undo a sin."

Anekand then visited his physicist self.

"So, you solved the problem! And you remember both realities?" said the physicist.

"Yes," Anekand said, and told him who the murderer was and how that same man helped him.

"I want to learn this art of making the leaps to other universes," said the physicist after listening to the story. "Will you teach me?"

"Yes. Of course," said Anekand. "You and some other Anekand's. And then the multiple us can meet sometime in some universe."

"Sure," said the physicist, "but we shall leave out the Kushala's."

They both laughed an oddly similar laugh.

www.ingramcontent.com/pod-product-compliance
Lightning Source LLC
Chambersburg PA
CBHW021012180726
47993CB00019B/2558